Yoruba Girl Dancing

SIMI BEDFORD

PENGUIN BOOKS

PENGUIN BOOKS
Published by the Penguin Group
Penguin Books USA Inc., 375 Hudson Street, New York, New York 10014, U.S.A.
Penguin Books Ltd, 27 Wrights Lane, London W8 5TZ, England
Penguin Books Australia Ltd, Ringwood, Victoria, Australia
Penguin Books Canada Ltd, 10 Alcorn Avenue, Toronto, Ontario, Canada M4V 3B2
Penguin Books (N.Z.) Ltd, 182-190 Wairau Road, Auckland 10, New Zealand

Penguin Books Ltd, Registered Offices: Harmondsworth, Middlesex, England

First published in Great Britain by William Heinemann Limited 1991
First published in the United States of America by Viking Penguin,
a division of Penguin Books USA Inc., 1992
Published in Penguin Books 1994

7 9 10 8 6

THE LIBRARY OF CONGRESS HAS CATALOGUED THE HARDCOVER AS FOLLOWS:
Bedford, Simi.
Yoruba girl dancing/Simi Bedford.
p.   cm.
ISBN 0-670-84045-9 (hc.)
ISBN 0 14 02.3293 1 (pbk.)
I. Title.
PR9387.9.B44Y67   1992
823'.914—dc20   92–53783

Printed in the United States of America
Set in Palatino

PENGUIN BOOKS

YORUBA GIRL DANCING

Simi Bedford, born in Africa, was a model and
now writes for television and film. She has three
children and lives in London.

To my mother and father

– Chapter 1 –

'Africans can talk oh!' Aunt Rose often said.

She was right, in our house we spoke four languages, and two of them were English, loudly from morning till night, so it was a mystery to us, the foster children and me, that Grandma and Grandpa never spoke to each other at all. It was a mystery too that I didn't wake up dead every morning, because unless I was cross with her, I slept with Grandma in her big brass bed. There were twelve pillows on it, six on either side, and if I hadn't slept practically standing up, spreadeagled against them with my head angled back over the top one for air, I would have suffocated for sure under the covers.

Grandma was asleep; I liked to look at her in the morning when she was sleeping, because then her eyes were tight shut. When they were open they were black and shiny like pebbles under water and knew what you were thinking. Her face was smooth and peaceful. I stroked her white hair, soft as duck down, back from her forehead and tugged at her plait but she didn't wake up; so I left her and ran next door to my nurse Patience and she dressed me. I was ready and waiting in my grandmother's sitting room for James when he arrived to escort me up to breakfast on the top floor. James was Grandpa's steward.

'Well madam, I see you ready,' he said, knocking on Grandma's bedroom door, which was in the right-hand corner of the sitting room.

'Can we go now?' I was impatient to leave this morning, I had a choice piece of news.

'Yes yes, we dey go now,' he replied, laughing down at me.

'Do I look pretty?'

'You are fine, fine,' he said, as always.

Grandma's arm, plump and sepia coloured, appeared around the door with a white note folded in her hand and James plucked it from her fingers, sketched a small bow to the rest of her invisible behind the door and ushered me out in front of him.

Grandpa was already in his armchair sorting through his post, which scattered onto the floor as, taking a running jump, I settled myself in his lap and lay back against his shirt front which appeared dazzlingly white in the darkened room. I had hoped for a glimpse of Grandma's note – Grandpa had taught me to read when I was three – but he raised his arms above my head and read the letter safely out of reach. Frustrated, I slipped from his knee to fetch the Bible, which I'd left on the table next to his desk the day before, I didn't expect to find it there though, because both table and desk were heaped with books. The walls of Grandpa's sitting room were painted cream but you couldn't see them either, they were lined with books filling the shelves from floor to ceiling. Books spilled out of the shelves ruckling up the rugs on the polished wooden floor, vying for space with mounds of newspapers and periodicals, old and new. I found the Bible on the floor at the same time as a shout of laughter from Grandpa signalled that he'd come to the end of Grandma's note and brought James's head enquiringly around the door of the next room, where he was busy preparing breakfast. Hopefully I turned around too, but the joke was not to be shared.

'Come here,' Grandpa said and hugged me close so that my nose was filled with the scent of his cologne and coconut hair pomade. 'Where did we finish yesterday?'

We were working our way day by day through the Old Testament, Grandpa had little truck with the New, that the meek should inherit the earth had no place in his philosophy.

'God killed all the firstborn,' I said, opening the Bible with the green leather marker, 'and the Pharaoh was just about to let all the Israelites go.'

Frankly I thought the Pharaoh had brought his troubles on

himself. Moses had told him in no uncertain terms that unless he was allowed to lead the Israelites out of Egypt, God would smite every firstborn in the land and Pharaoh had been given plenty of proof with the nine plagues already visited on him that God would keep his word. It was horrifying all the same, though, because, as I pointed out to Grandpa, that would have been me, I was the firstborn child in my family. Grandpa assured me he would not have allowed it to happen. I believed him, he would have made a deal and got the best of it.

'Begin now!' he said, gesturing towards the page.

Keeping my place by moving my forefinger carefully beneath each word, I began reading. But Grandpa was not in the mood; no sooner were the Israelites safely across the Red Sea and the pursuing Egyptians drowned in their chariots, than he called out to James that we were ready to eat.

I wasn't ready to let the Israelites go just yet though. I waited until James had finished wrapping me in a big white napkin in order to protect my dress and then I said, 'Aunt Rose says that we used to be slaves, like the Israelites.'

'Aunt Rose talks too much. What will you eat?'

'Did we, Grandpa?'

He spooned up his pawpaw and didn't answer; after a pause and another mouthful, he said testily, 'Yes, in America, but that was a long time ago. The important thing for you to remember is that our family came back.'

'To Lagos?'

'Not initially, they settled in Sierra Leone to begin with.'

'Where Uncle Marcus and lots of the cousins live?'

'That's right. Are you not eating this morning?'

'Were you a slave, Grandpa?'

'Of course not! Do I look like a slave? However it is a fact that my grandfather was one. You know he was a very brave man: he fought, along with many other slaves, on the side of the British in their war against the Americans and in return for his help he was given his freedom. Afterwards the British brought all the freed slaves to Sierra Leone. They crossed the Atlantic Ocean in a big ship and it arrived just in time for my father, your great-grandfather, Elias Foster, to be born a free man in Africa again. When he became a grown man he came home: to Nigeria. He settled in Lagos and began trading in palm oil. He was very successful too.'

'Like Moses!'

'Exactly.'

'How did great-grandpa Elias know that this was his home?'

'Well he knew that according to our family tradition we came originally from the area around Abeokuta, so he made a journey up there and when he arrived he immediately recognised the tribal markings on the faces of the people, they were identical to the pattern handed down to his father by his grandfather in America. We are home for good now, I promise you.'

'I don't think I'd like to go to America.'

'But you would like to go to England some day, wouldn't you, to study?'

'Like Papa and Aunt Harriet? Some day maybe.'

'Now! What are you going to eat?'

I looked at the bowl on the table, it was hard to choose from the mangoes, pawpaws, guavas, oranges, pineapple, grapefruit and melon. I asked James, who'd been standing by, to cut me an avocado in half and sprinkle it with salt. We ate in silence and it wasn't until I was halfway through my second slice of pineapple – I loved pineapple – that I remembered my news for Grandpa. I felt sorry for Grandpa – he never knew anything, because he only ever left his eyrie to go to the Chamber of Commerce and to church on Sunday.

'Sisi Bola's getting married,' I said, looking at him sideways.

'Don't speak with your mouth full. Who is she marrying?'

'Akin Ojo.'

Grandpa raised his eyebrows, 'She only recently left for England, are you sure?'

'Oh yes. She came back last week and Nimota says – you know my nurse Nimota? – she says that it must have been love at first look.'

Grandpa roared with laughter. 'Indeed.'

'And Patience says – '

'Which one is Patience?'

'Grandpa you know my nurse Patience very well.'

'Do I?'

'Yes! She says that the food in England have plenty magic, because Sisi Bola only stick out de back when she go, but she stick out the front too like a elephant when she come back.'

My grandfather laughed again. 'You are a disgraceful child! Eat up, eat up now.'

'Don't you want to know when the wedding is?'

'I'm sure you will tell me.'

'It's in three weeks' time. I'm to be a bridesmaid. Aunt Delma has asked Grandma.'

Aunt Delma was Grandma's sister and Sisi Bola's mother.

Sisi Bola was to be married from our house and Aunt Rose said that Aunt Delma was exceedingly lucky to have a sister like Grandma who was not only generous but who was also wife to the richest man in Lagos. The wedding, she said, would be the wedding of the decade, we should mark her words. I repeated this to Yowande, the youngest of the foster children, who, although three years older than me, was my best friend in the house. She didn't know what wedding of the decade meant either, but she did know that Nimota, my second nanny, was planning to put a curse on Yetunde, her rival in love, so that she would be too sick to attend any of the celebrations. I must be careful not to say anything, she said, because if Grandma found out she would beat us all.

'I won't tell her,' I said. Yowande looked sceptical. It wasn't fair, just because I was the youngest in the house. Even I knew how fanatical Grandma was about that kind of thing. She considered it a blasphemy against the Christian Religion. And anyway I never told tales now.

We all, the Fosters that is, lived a stone's throw from the Marina in the residential area off Broad Street: Broad Street, Aunt Rose said, was the commercial centre, whatever that meant, of Lagos, where, she said, men of substance like Grandpa had built their mansions in the European style. Nimota said that that simply meant Grandpa was a big man. Where she came from, up country, he would have been, she said, a Paramount Chief. It was a fact that Grandpa's warehouses, which we passed nearly every day on our constitutional along the Marina, stretched for half a mile around the bay, I'd been inside many times of course with Grandpa. Aunt Rose, who frequently accompanied Nimota and me, said that Grandpa's warehouses were filled with all the riches of the continent, but actually they contained quite ordinary everyday things, as Grandpa said. Palm oil, leather, timber and stuff like that. You name it, Aunt Rose said, and Grandpa sold it. He had branches and factories throughout the country, even where Nimota came from, and that was very remote. Aunt Rose counted them up on her fingers, there were twenty-three in all, branches, that is, not fingers, Aunt Rose had the normal number, but you wouldn't think so, Nimota said, they were into everything. Our house was four storeys high and painted a bright strawberry pink with a cream pattern of whirls and fancy flourishes around the windows and doors. The Lagos sun which, Grandma said, can wreak such havoc with pink complexions, had been kind to this one and aged it gently, so that with time the colour had mellowed and become discreet. Long rows of windows each with its own wrought-iron balcony looked out across the front, and large double doors opened directly onto the street. At the back there was a large paved courtyard with a well in the centre. A huge avocado provided shade, as did the mango, pawpaw, guava and banana trees; broad-leaved ferns masked the hot glitter of the paving stones. During the day we liked to sit pleasantly and peacefully, on the benches under the trees; the light filtering down through the leaves was always green and forest cool. At night the courtyard was lit by the fires of the servants cooking their food in the outside kitchen and loud with the sound of crickets. The smoke from the fires kept the mosquitoes at bay.

We were a miniature village, thirty people lived in our house. Grandpa lived on the top floor and was attended by his own servants. He and Grandma had been effectively separated for fifteen years; he never came downstairs. Even so he ruled us all, his word was law and his power was absolute. Aunt Rose said that people were equally terrified of him outside the house, including the score of Europeans he employed. I heard her tell Patience that she herself was so in awe of him she had only dared to address him directly three or four times in the twenty years since she had been living under his roof. I thought that was pretty silly of Aunt Rose. I wasn't scared of Grandpa and he certainly wasn't frightening to look at. The neat whorls of his hair had turned to grey, but his moustache was marvellously black and glossy and so was his skin which had an almost metallic sheen. It seemed to me that he was always laughing and, unlike Grandma, who complained of the smell that clung to me when I came back down after breakfast upstairs, I liked his cigars. He was seldom without one, either clenched in his teeth or drifting smoke from between his long fingers. It was all right for me, Aunt Rose said, I was the favoured grandchild, the little princess.

My grandmother, Grandma Loretta, ruled the rest of the household from her sitting room, which served as another courtyard inside the house. All the other rooms on the first floor opened onto it. Stationed in her rocking chair in the corner by her bedroom door, no coming or going escaped her notice. I loved Grandma, she was fat and marvellously comfortable to sit on, her brown skin was soft to touch and she wore her hair plaited in a crown around her head. Any impression of cosiness however was dispelled by a second glance at her eyes, it was impossible to look into them and lie.

With the exception of my father Simon, all Grandpa and Grandma's children were still living at home. My father Simon was the eldest and my Aunt Harriet was next. In fact, however, they were not Grandma's children at all: they were Grandpa's two children by the Fante princess. So she was my real grandmother, but I never knew her, she was never seen in Lagos and she died in Ghana which was her country long before I was born. Grandma brought up the two children as if they were her own. Aunt Harriet, who resembled her mother and kept a photograph of her locked in her drawer, was considered a great beauty. The photograph showed a magnificent woman with bare shoulders wrapped in a length of Kente cloth, which, so Aunt Harriet told me and I told Yowande, could only be worn by royalty. If the picture were in colour the cloth would be glowing red, green and gold, like the stained-glass windows in Lagos cathedral. Her jet black hair was pulled up in a fan shape over a wooden frame and fastened with solid gold nuggets as befitted a Fante princess. Grandma said, and I heard her say it many times to Aunt Rose when they were sitting taking a glass of home-made ginger beer, that though Aunt Harriet, who was a barrister, was brilliant, she was too highly strung. Grandma was worried that Harriet might even be a little unstable. After all it was common knowledge that there was . . . well, instability, in the Fante princess's family. There was no denying Aunt Harriet was sensitive, because as Aunt Rose said, she had a habit of bursting into tears at the least little thing and rushing from the room.

Aunt Sylvia, Grandma's own elder daughter, was brilliant too, she was going to be a doctor. As Aunt Rose said, making sure that Grandma heard her, there was nothing unstable about that one. She was my father's favourite, he liked to hold her up as a perfect model of African womanhood. According to my father Aunt Sylvia was serious, clever, modest and good. Nobody was perfect, Aunt Rose said. Aunt Grace, the youngest of my father's brothers and sisters, was my favourite, Yowande and I loved to play with her hair which was thick and shoulder length and watch her maid straighten-ing it and curling it in the latest styles from England. Aunt Grace's eyebrows were two perfect arches, she was destined to be a film star. We knew it.

Grandma's only son Uncle George would normally have been at home too, but he had gone to England to fly aeroplanes and fight in the war. According to Patience he was a source of great pride, anger and anxiety for my grand-mother, not necessarily in that order. Opinion in the house was divided about Uncle George: we children thought he was a hero but Aunt Rose, and Patience too, believed he was downright foolhardy to get involved in dem white people war. They didn't say this to Grandma. Everyone had to be careful too on the subject of Uncle Henry. He was Grandpa's son by an outside wife and the spitting image of Grandpa. Yowande and I knew from listening to conversations around the house (we had our eyes to every keyhole and our ear to every door, Aunt Rose said, but she was no better, in Nimota's opinion) that Uncle Henry was one of the reasons Grandma never spoke to Grandpa, but no one explained why. Aunt Rose would only say that certain tenets of the Christian faith appealed to Grandpa more than others and one man one wife was not among them.

Aunt Rose had been living with my grandparents for twenty years, ever since she had arrived for a short holiday in her teens. Even the servants referred to her as poor Aunt Rose, not because she was a poor relation, which she was, but because she had never married, and even worse, Nimota said, she had no children. She was given to wearing dark coloured dresses with pale collars; thin and spindly, she hugged the corners of the house, delicate yet durable, like a cobweb.

Aunt Sylvia said that we made Aunt Rose's life intolerable. There were ten of us, nine foster children and me. The foster children were the sons and daughters of poor relations, like Aunt Rose; their parents sent them to live in Grandpa's house so that they could advance themselves. Yowande was the youngest, she was nine; Morenike was the eldest, she was fifteen and would be going home soon. In fact she would be leaving the CMS just as I was beginning. Alaba who was my third nanny would miss her most, they were the same age. Aunt Rose said that when one of the foster children left, another appeared to take its place, miraculously, like shark's teeth. And then there was me: everybody knew who I was. I was Remi Foster, the eldest of Simon Foster's three children, and Grandpa and Grandma's first grandchild. I lived with them because, as Grandpa said, Grandma would have been sad without a baby growing up in the house, and so would he. I was on permanent loan: it was the custom with the eldest grandchild and anyway, as Aunt Rose said, I was only a girl. She also said that no child required three nannies to trail after her all day long. I would be spoiled for life, we should mark her words. Well, the foster children certainly didn't spoil me, if

I told tales they beat me up, and Grandma beat me too just to be sure. My life wasn't easy, like Aunt Rose thought. I couldn't tell her though, my lips were sealed.

'Where have you been?' Yowande wanted to know. She was out of breath. 'I couldn't find you anywhere.'

'Around.'

'Nimota's looking for you.' She winked heavily and nudged me in my side.

'Why?'

Yowande winked again. 'You remember,' she said. 'I told you, she wants to buy a spell. I heard her tell Alaba that today was the day.'

'Ah!' I said, winking heavily and nudging her back. I remembered that Nimota wanted a curse for Yetunde. 'Where is she?'

'Looking for you, come on.'

We both hurried up the ouside staircase into the house. Nimota was waiting in the conservatory at the top.

'Come, change your dress, we are going out.'

'But it is not time for my walk yet,' I said.

'Just you do as I say and be quick about it. You hear me?'

Yowande giggled.

'You want me to beat you oh!' Nimota took a step towards her. Yowande disappeared.

'Where are you going?' Grandma said when we reappeared in her sitting room on our way out and she saw me changed into a new dress. 'It's early for her walk.'

'We are going the long way round today, Ma.' Nimota dropped a little customary curtsey when talking to Grandma.

'Come here, child!' I skipped across to her in her rocking chair and leant my elbows in her lap, with my chin resting on my hands.

'Yes Grandma?' I said, looking up.

'Turn around.' She straightened my belt and smoothed my plaits down with both her hands. 'You be good.'

'Where are we going?' I asked Nimota.

We had been walking for a long time taking shortcuts through unfamiliar back streets and I was afraid we were lost.

'We are going to Jankara market. You will like it,' Nimota said, keeping up the pace. I was exhausted.

Jankara market was in the Isaleko district and was very rough. Grandma would be appalled if she knew I'd been there: neither she nor my aunts would have dreamt of going there.

'Grandma will be very angry,' I said as we reached the outskirts of the market.

'Who is going to tell her?' Nimota stopped short, causing me to bump into her. She placed her hands on her hips and leant her head on one side.

'Not me,' I said.

'Aha. You better stick my back like flea.' She sailed forward once again.

I hurriedly took hold of the back of her skirt and my arm went whipping from side to side with the roll of her hips. Down the centre aisle we went, past the fish stalls, past the grain sheds and the meat and vegetables; straight on through the fancy goods, turning left by the pots and pans, and then right where the bales of cloth were protected from the sun under canopies.

We were deaf to the loud enticements of the market women, and to the last hopeless squawks of the chickens flapping underfoot.

Nimota's pace did not slacken until we passed the last of the stalls and had to pick our way carefully around clumps of slippery debris already rotting in the burning sun. I let go her skirt and rubbed my shoulder in relief, my arm felt as if it had been pulled out at the root. Unwisely I drew in a deep breath and spat it out again quickly, ugh, as the unexpectedly putrid smell hit the inside of my head.

'Nimota, I want to go home,' I said.

'Make we go on now,' she said, very sharply.

I made no further protest. I disagreed with Nimota on lots of subjects: for one thing I didn't think that she should put a curse on Yetunde, it seemed to me that she could quite well manage to keep Kemi for herself, she was bigger and stronger than both he and Yetunde. On the other hand a curse was better than killing her, I suppose, because I had overheard Nimota tell Patience, 'If I go catch her with Kemi, I go kill am, so better stop her before.' The curse would be a kindness really. And for another thing, Yetunde did not have a squint – Yowande and I thought she was quite pretty. In this instance, though, I did agree that having come we should press on as quickly as possible so as not to arouse Grandma's suspicions.

We came to a stop in front of a row of lean-tos.

'Wait here.'

In one swift movement, without giving me a chance to disobey, Nimota removed my hand once more from the back of her dress and disappeared into the darkness of the nearest hut.

A group of girls had trailed us all the way through the market; now they had me cornered and there was not a grown-up in sight. There was a drain in between us, thank goodness. They'd have a problem crossing over, I thought. The planks were very slippery, and they were hampered by the babies they carried on their hips. Frustrated, they started to taunt me.

'Oyinbo, oyinbo,' they shouted, calling me white because they had heard Nimota speaking to me in English.

'I am not so,' I shouted back in Yoruba.

We stared at each other transfixed, I by their raggedness and near nakedness, and they by my leather shoes and the English smocking on my dress.

When she could bear it no longer, the biggest of the girls decided to come across anyway, and to my horror, still carrying her baby brother, she waded barefoot into the slime and began slipping and sliding her way towards me, making the water brim over the sides. Close up she wasn't frightening, however, and her hand was lightly tracing the embroidery on my bodice when Nimota emerged from the hut blinking and shading her eyes. She pulled me away and the contact was broken.

On the way back I asked Nimota what was going to happen to Yetunde. Her consultation with Mama Ibeji must have been successful because in place of an answer she just smiled. She made me promise not to breathe a word to anybody of where we'd been or why. If I did, she said, she'd skin me alive.

– Chapter 2 –

Aunt Delma and Sisi Bola, who had been coming to the house every day, moved in. They were not the only ones, some relatives from out of town arrived early.

'We are already doubling up downstairs,' I told Grandpa at breakfast, 'but you've plenty of room up here.'

'Already, surely not! And who says I've plenty of room?'

'Grandma says. She said that when everybody's here the children will have to stay upstairs with you.'

'Good God, am I to have no sleep as well as every other inconvenience? As I recall on the last occasion your parents visited us, your baby sister screamed non-stop at the top of her extraordinarily powerful lungs.'

'Not us children; Grandma wants us near her, she means your children: Aunt Harriet, Sylvia, Grace and Uncle Henry. And Grandma says you're lucky, you only have to pay.'

Grandpa's laughter shook his whole body. 'Did you hear that, James?' he said, wiping his face with his napkin.

'Yes, sah,' said James who was standing by behind Grandpa's chair.

'Aunt Rose has already moved out of her room.'

'What does she say?'

'She says you can well afford it.'

Mopping his eyes again, this time with a large pocket handkerchief, Grandpa said, 'It's almost worth it, I hope you are all having as much fun down there as I am up here.'

'Oh we are! We're having our final fittings today and choosing the asoebi. The bridesmaids' dresses are in damask rose silk, did you know that? And the pages are all going to be wearing cream silk shirts and brown velvet breeches. Aunt Delma asked Aunt Grace to choose the colours – Aunt Grace is very good with colours, everybody says so. She wants to study art you know. Grandpa, you really should come and see for yourself.'

'Aunt Grace wants to study art, does she? Well well. No, my dear, I won't come down. I have excitement enough hearing it all from you.'

'I have to go now, Grandpa, Grandma says there are a million things to do and she needs my help this morning.'

'Very well. Give me a kiss before you go. I think,' he said, looking round at James, 'that we might be able to manage with less space for a short time, don't you?'

'Yes, sah!'

'I'll tell Grandma,' I said.

'Thank you, madam,' Grandpa said. 'You're too kind.'

Aunt Grace was in charge and she twirled around the room unrolling first one bale of cloth and then another, now holding up this length, first against herself and each of us in turn. Tonight, she said, we should imagine ourselves in an Eastern Bazaar. The Indian ladies who had brought round the materials for us to see from their shop on the Marina, giggled behind their hands at this and their gold bangles tinkled. Patience said it looked more like Jankara market to her. At that I nudged Yowande and looked at Nimota who was looking daggers at me.

'The child is in her element,' Grandma said, her eyes on Aunt Grace.

We were all present. Grandma had called everyone into her sitting room on the first floor. Aunt Sylvia and Aunt Harriet sat side by side next to Aunt Rose; Grandma was in her rocking chair in the corner by her bedroom door, her usual place; the Indian ladies fluttered beside her, their saris lifting gently in the breeze from the fans, turning overhead. Yowande and I sat crosslegged at Grandma's feet, Sisi Bola and Aunt Delma occupied the sofa opposite, with Morenike and Alaba on one side and Patience and Nimota on the other on the floor. Tea and homemade gingerbeer were the order of the day, which the maids passed around. The floor in the middle was piled high with bales of cloth, damask and silk, gold and silver tissue, moire and lace covered every available surface in the sitting room, the little sitting room and the long dining room visible through the big double doors on either side.

Aunt Grace finished her parade and Grandma invited suggestions as to which, of the myriad materials spread before us, we should adopt for the family asoebi. We would be wearing it for the African celebrations and dancing, which would take place in the evening of Sisi Bola's wedding day. Asoebi was the Yoruba custom whereby all the women in each family were dressed in identical cloth so that at any gathering you could tell at a glance who belonged to whom. These festivities would follow the ceremony in Lagos cathedral in the morning and the European-style wedding breakfast in the afternoon. Our family, coming from Sierra Leone, blended both traditions happily.

'How will we choose?' Yowande whispered.

As if reading her thoughts, Aunt Harriet suggested that we put it to the vote.

'Here, here.' Aunt Sylvia looked up from her book; so as not to waste a moment away from her studies, she had brought some reading with her.

'I think Aunt Grace should choose,' I said.

There was a shocked silence.

'That child is a disgrace,' Aunt Rose said.

'Come up here,' Grandma commanded. I climbed up onto her knee. 'Do not say another word. Mice must be silent and still, or they will be crushed.'

I lay back, anchored on the slippery silk of her lap with my fingers hooked into the neck of her dress. It was deliciously cool against my face and I wondered, not for the first time, why, next to her skin, Grandma always wore six red flannel petticoats. Much of life was a mystery, I thought before I fell asleep lulled by the rocking of her chair.

Yowande told me that in the end, to nobody's surprise,

Grandma had chosen the material. The Foster women would all be wearing pink with a gold thread. She also said, 'You're for it: she knows.'

'What does she know?' I said in alarm. 'That the boys put the frogs in Aunt Rose's bed? I didn't tell her.'

'No, worse than that, Ma has found out about the spell, Aunt Delma told her.'

My heart was pounding. 'I didn't tell her.'

'You must have told someone.'

I remembered that I might have mentioned it to Ebun Ogunsola, who was to be another of the bridesmaids, when she came for her fitting.

'She must have told her mother and she told Aunt Delma,' Yowande said.

I looked around fearfully in case Grandma should appear and, seeing nobody about, Yowande and I dashed outside down the stairs and slunk across the courtyard where the boys were noisily practising their dance steps. We slumped down behind the trunk of the avocado tree and Yowande, who was brilliant that way, pulled out a handful of chinchin pastries from her pocket which we munched for comfort.

Grandma hated heathenism. She said it was the mark of the savage and that superstitious practices by which we all knew she meant juju would on no account be tolerated in our house. She was very religious and so was Aunt Rose, who said that Sierra Leonians were more religious than other people. This was probably true, because we went to church three times on Sunday if you counted Sunday school, not to mention bible reading and prayers twice with Grandma downstairs and then once again with Grandpa upstairs. Aunt Harriet and Aunt Sylvia were very religious too because they kept their eyes tight shut when they were praying and didn't look around to see what everybody else was doing. Aunt Grace said that Sierra Leonians went to church to show their hats off like everybody else. Aunt Sylvia disagreed: Africans, she said, were a deeply spiritual people. Aunt Grace said you wouldn't have thought so if you had been a fly on the wall in Lagos cathedral last Sunday when the final banns for Sisi Bola and Akin Ojo's marriage were read.

The cathedral certainly had been packed, it was very hot and we were all sweating, even though the cathedral was in a nice breezy place: facing out across the Marina, with Odulami Street on one side and shady cloisters on the other, which looked out onto a green space planted with tall palm trees. Our Sunday procession to church had been longer than normal: there had been four cars; Grandpa of course in the first car all by himself, and I was in the second with Grandma and my aunts, other relatives crowded into the third and fourth cars, with the foster children and the servants as usual walking behind. The Foster pew was right in the front so you had a good view but I was wedged in very tightly between Grandma and Aunt Sylvia and I couldn't look around so I studied the ceiling instead. I had never noticed before that the columns looked like the palm trees outside with curving stone branches fanning out in all directions, holding up the roof. The light streaming in through the stained glass windows was coloured green and red. When we stood up to praise the Lord you couldn't help but see that everyone was in their best clothes and the latest hats from Paris; showing off what Aunt Grace called their serious jewellery.

Aunt Rose said that she had to admit that there was some truth in what Aunt Grace said and that some Lagos people were not as serious as they ought to be about religion. She said that Bishop Wilson-Harris must have thought so too last Sunday or he wouldn't have seized the opportunity to take as the text for his sermon, that it was easier for a camel to pass through the needle's eye than for a rich man to enter the Kingdom of Heaven. Grandma said he was an old hypocrite, he was perfectly happy for Grandpa to pay for his niece's wedding!

Still, Aunt Rose said, surely God would allow some rich people to enter the Kingdom of Heaven, it would be a sad place without them. Whereupon Grandma wondered, as a matter of interest, just how many people from Warri succeeded in gaining entry, whatever their status. Warri was Aunt Rose's home town.

Cousin Yemi, who was eight, summed up neatly (we had a

houseful back for Sunday lunch) when he said, 'No one is rich when they arrive in heaven, Grandma, because they can't take their money with them, can they?'

Grandma said that children should be seen and not heard, but she'd smiled at his mother.

'Another lawyer in the making,' Aunt Sylvia had said.

Retribution was not long in coming. Grandma summoned us before her. We stood in a large semicircle around her rocking chair: all the foster children, my two young nannies and me. Yowande stood next to me but we didn't look at each other. The fans whirred overhead and a warm breeze blew in through the windows of the dining room, bringing with it the delicious smell of chillies frying and corn roasting outside in the courtyard. Ordinarily this would have set our mouths watering but our stomachs were still queasy from the dose of castor oil Grandma administered once a week to flush out worms. Desperate to avoid our compulsory medication, we had all, without exception, enrolled in the Lagos Boy Scouts and Girl Guides, because their meetings conflicted with Grandma's timing; you couldn't have both. When Yowande and I paraded for Aunt Grace and Aunt Sylvia in our new uniforms and told them we were Rosebuds now, as Nigerian Brownies were called, Aunt Grace offended us both by laughing. Although she apologised and said she wasn't laughing at us, she laughed even louder when we explained some of the Guide rules. A Guide obeys orders, a Guide is a friend to animals, a Guide smiles and sings under all difficulties, a Guide is pure in thought, word and deed. A Guide is . . .

'Stop, stop,' she said, 'did you tell Miss Emmerson why you all joined?'

Miss Emmerson was a pretty English lady and our Captain.

'No, of course not,' we said.

Aunt Sylvia laughed too then, which was surprising.

'It was a nice paradigm,' she said, 'of the colonial relationship at work.' Aunt Sylvia liked to use difficult words. Aunt Grace said it was because she was going to be a doctor.

It did us no good, Grandma simply changed her timing.

'We are Christians in this house!' Her voice cracked over us now like a whip and her eyes raked the circle; we kept our eyes down, if you might have to lie to Grandma it was best not to look at her. 'That is the religion we practise and I will not tolerate any other.'

'Yes, Grandma.'

'You are all saying yes when I know for a fact that someone of you has attempted to bring juju in here. I want to know who; here and now!'

We remained silent. Grandma allowed the silence to lengthen, then she said, 'I called all of you because I want to make sure that you all understand my mind on this matter. However I am reasonably certain on this occasion that the boys are not guilty. You may go.'

The boys filed out and we shuffled round to form a straight line.

'You, Nimota, stand forward. I have reason to believe that you are the guilty party.'

'No, Ma.'

'Don't lie to me. You have been to consult Mama Ibeji, not so?'

'Yes, Ma.'

'You admit it?'

We looked in disbelief at Nimota.

She said, 'No, Ma. I say, yes I no go lie to you.'

'Did you or did you not go?' Grandma shouted in exasperation.

'No, Ma.'

Our eyes swivelled in unison back to Grandma.

'You, Alaba? Morenike? Yetunde? Yowande?' She asked each of them in turn.

'No,' they said.

Grandma turned to me.

'Come here,' she said silkily.

'Did Nimota take you to the market?'

'Jankara market, Grandma?'

'Yes, Jankara market.'

'No.'

'How did you know I meant Jankara market then?'

I didn't answer. Grandma was silent. Our eyes glanced surreptitiously towards the two long switches, tapering to a fine flexible point and placed at her right hand against the wall.

'As none of you is prepared to tell me the truth I shall beat all of you.'

Grandma beat me last. If I learnt my lesson now, she said, I would not forget it. The switch snaked down six times on my outstretched palm, the pain was insupportable; tears pouring down my cheeks I ran next door to Patience, who was waiting with Nimota.

'Damn fool!' Patience said, rocking me in her arms and rubbing my palm, which was on fire. 'Why you go take de pickin?'

'I go take am for protection, I tink Ma no go punish if she knew de child involve in de ting. Sorry oh,' she said, taking me into her arms while Patience prepared the bed. My hand smarted all night.

My parents were the last to arrive in Lagos for the wedding. They had a long way to travel since my father, who was a magistrate, was on a tour of duty way out in the east. Yowande and I were both very impressed by the fact that he could put people in prison. Yowande had been angry with me for a while after the beating because she reckoned that I had given the game away by letting slip the name of Jankara market. She wasn't able to be angry with me for long though because she knew that I would ask to be taken to play with Ebun Ogunsola (who had caused all the trouble in the first place by telling Aunt Delma) or my other special friend, also to be a bridesmaid, Derin McKenzie. It was Yowande who came rushing out to the courtyard where Alaba was reading me the Snow Queen, one of my favourite fairy stories, under the mango trees, to tell me they'd arrived. It was difficult to imagine snow.

I exploded into my mother's room like a firecracker and she jumped up and caught me in her arms. Putting me down, she

21

said, 'Turn around, let me look at you.' Obligingly I spun around, my skirt flying out in a bell. 'Come here.' She sat down again in her chair, I ran and leant against her knees and looked up laughing at her face. She inspected me minutely, but said only, 'You've grown.'

'My hair has grown too,' I said, holding out a plait for her inspection.

She kissed me. 'I do hope you have been behaving yourself.'

I drew away. 'Yes,' I lied airily, 'I always do.'

I looked around the room; my mother had not finished unpacking and her clothes were strewn all over the bed on top of the Indian counterpane. I liked the pattern, great big flowers and birds, but not like any you'd ever see, painted in blue on a cream background. The walls were cream too, most of the walls in our house were painted cream. There were Indian rugs too on the floor but they were hidden for the moment under the travelling cases which were lying open in the middle of the room. There were more dresses draped over the linen-covered armchairs and Patience, who was helping my mother to unpack, carefully shook the folds out of each one before she transferred it to the wardrobe in the dressing room next door. Then I looked towards the windows. They stretched from floor to ceiling and were left ajar at this time of day, but both the shaded balconies beyond were empty. I was surprised – were was my brother?

'Where is Tunji?'

'Here I am.'

I looked behind my mother's chair and there he was, with his great big eyes and sticking out ears. I grinned at him; his head always seemed too heavy for his neck and wobbled at times as if it might fall off. I hauled him out – he was rather shy at first when he arrived in Lagos after an absence – and we ran for the door.

'Don't you want to see the baby?'

'Yes, Mama, soon,' I called out over my shoulder; there were more important things to see to outside.

We stopped to kiss Grandma in her rocking chair, as we

passed by. I'd gone back to Grandma's bed the very next night after she beat me; Grandma, after all, was to me like breathing and you didn't question her behaviour any more than you did the weather. I produced my brother with a flourish at the top of the courtyard stairs.

'Look!' I said to Yowande, pulling Tunji down behind me. 'We have a partner now for the dancing.'

'I suppose he's better than nothing,' Yowande said doubtfully as we fell into step beside her.

I didn't see my father until it was time for bed, he and my mother were taking coffee with Grandma after supper. Holding me at arm's length, he said to my mother, 'She has not grown any prettier,' and to me, 'Where are your shoes?'

'I don't know, Papa.'

'Have you lost them?'

'No, Papa.'

'Go and put them on at once.'

'But, Papa, I am on my way to bed.'

'Simon, you haven't seen the child for three months,' my mother protested.

'That is no reason for her not to wear her shoes,' he replied.

'Yes, Papa,' I said and hurried from the room. It was no good trying to please my father, he was too disappointed that his first child had been born a girl. Everybody said so.

Lit up for Sisi Bola's Spinster's Eve, our house seemed to be floating in the darkness. My brother and I were acting as unofficial greeters outside in the street, and as each of the guests arrived, we rushed ahead of them up the stairs, tripping over our clothes and theirs in our excitement, to announce their names to the others already in the sitting room.

Aunt Rose who was by the door shook her head and said, 'They go tire before de party begin. Mark my words.'

She was, like everyone else, sitting on a chair set against the walls and facing inwards. Unlike everyone else though, she had chosen to remain in European dress: she was wearing one of her dark blue frocks and the long points of her collar gave her a forlorn look like the picture in my book of a circus dog with its head pushed through a paper hoop. To be fair, Aunt Rose couldn't have competed with all the gold thread, silver tissue and lace covering the spread knees and bosoms, some of them as big as Grandma's, of the women gathered here. Even Grandma had abandoned her silk dresses for this night and was wearing full Yoruba costume. Aunt Grace had tied her headdress for her in a magnificent turban that would have aroused the envy of an Indian maharaja, Aunt Harriet said. It was in the same blue material as her blouse and richly embroidered with gold, and so was her ero, worn wrapped around like a skirt and then knotted at the waist, her ipele which was bound tightly across her hips and the eborun, folded lengthwise and thrown over her shoulder. Her costume could have stood up on its own without Grandma.

Mama had dressed me in the Sierra Leonian 'up and down' that had only two pieces, a figure-hugging bodice, the 'up', and a skirt the 'down' which fitted just as tightly all the way to the ground. This was the style that the young women were wearing. Aunt Grace said it showed the figure off to perfection. Aunt Sylvia said that that was not the reason she had decided to wear it, she was wearing Sierra Leonian dress because it was very simple. To begin with I was happy to circulate with Grandma, holding on to her hand and towing her along like a tug bringing a barge into Lagos harbour, but I quickly tired of my self-appointed task and when Yowande came running in accompanied by shrieks of laughter from the dining room to tell me that the food was now all laid out on the table, I abandoned Grandma and we rushed away together through the double doors to investigate.

In the dining room, which ran the length of the house, every window was flung open onto the courtyard. Beneath, on a cushioned bench, Sisi Bola was sitting holding court, surrounded by her cousins and friends. Aunt Grace stood beside her leaning with her elbows back against the windowsill, while Aunt Sylvia and Aunt Harriet plied her with her favourite delicacies from the table in the centre. The table was covered with a white damask tablecloth and loaded to breaking point with food and drink. The sound of the fans was drowned out by the noise. Catching sight of us, Sisi Bola, who was small and round and was becoming each day, as Patience pointed out, noticeably rounder than before, called us over to her with an imperious wave of her hand. She looked like a married woman already, in pink lace and a turban to rival Grandma's.

'Remi,' she said, pressing my cheek to hers which was smooth and shiny as satin, 'we have been discussing love and marriage. When it is your turn who will you marry?'

'That's easy, I shall marry Grandpa,' I said firmly, provoking much laughter, then I said, looking sideways from Yowande to Sisi Bola, 'I know who Aunt Grace is going to marry.'

'Who is that?' Sisi Bola was delighted.

'Uncle Bode,' I said, this time provoking screams.

'Horrible, horrible child.' Aunt Grace, turning a richer shade of brown, leapt from her place. 'Wait until I catch you.'

But I was quicker. Snatching a cake, followed closely by Yowande, I fled through the conservatory and down the outside staircase into the courtyard where I hid behind my mother.

Grandpa said that my mother was the prettiest of us all, she reminded him of a forest gazelle. I thought so too. She was the most slender and her cheekbones were high and curved under her burnished copper skin and hair of deepest black. Aunt Sylvia, from a medical point of view, Aunt Harriet presumed, was puzzled how one so slim could comfortably accommodate all her internal organs.

'Hey, what is it,' my mother wanted to know, putting out a restraining arm as I hurled myself behind her chair.

'Aunt Grace is chasing me,' I said. 'She wants to beat me.'

'What have you done?'

'Nothing,' I said.

'Well you don't need to hide, come and sit here on my lap.'

And that's where Aunt Grace found me, in my mother's arms.

'That child,' she said, shaking her fist at me in mock anger, 'will come to a bad end.'

'I don't doubt it,' my mother said, laughing.

But I went looking for Aunt Grace again when the drumming started and the dancing began. Mama said I should dance with my brother, but he wasn't receiving the message of the music at all clearly.

'Tunji, not like that, bend your knees like this.'

He took no notice of me and continued wobbling his head to a different beat. He was going to let us down badly at the wedding. Yowande and I abandoned him to my mother and danced our way across the courtyard to join my aunts and their circle. The music poured through our veins and we flowed with the beat, each separate portion of our bodies winding and unwinding seamlessly as if we had no bones. Even Aunt Rose could not resist the pull of the drums and we surrounded her gleefully. 'That's right, Auntie, move it, move it, oh!'

We danced long into the night underneath the lanterns strung between the trees. Inside the house, the old ladies moved their chairs so that they could observe us, and sat looking out, framed like pictures in the dining room windows. 'No snake is more sinuous,' they said, 'than a Yoruba girl dancing.'

The train on Sisi Bola's wedding dress was very long, it seemed to me, and looked as if it might stretch the length of Lagos Cathedral. Fortunately there were six pages to take care of it, and the chief page was making sure they didn't make any mistakes today, which was just as well, because yesterday at the rehearsal Uncle Henry, who was in charge of all the arrangements, had had to reprimand them for playing the fool. The inside of the cathedral was barely recognisable; the whole place had been transformed with flowers twined around the pillars, which already had fruit and flowers carved on them. There was a capacity crowd just as there had been when the banns were read, but today there were crowds outside also waiting on the pavement. They cheered Sisi Bola when she arrived and they would still be waiting, I supposed, to see us leave. All the traffic in the centre of town had had to be redirected and the policeman on the roundabout saluted us smartly when we passed. Ebun and I saluted him back.

Ebun and I were side by side in the bride's procession. Uncle Henry put us in the middle with Derin because we were the three youngest; we were between the pages carrying the train and the three older bridesmaids, who could keep an eye on us, Uncle Henry said, bringing up the rear. Yesterday at supper, which we were allowed to stay up for, my father said to Uncle Henry that he hoped I wouldn't do anything to disgrace us all, and Uncle Henry said my father was unjust towards me. So far everything was going well. This morning when she saw her, Grandma said Sisi Bola's dress was a triumph, and Aunt Rose said, but not so Grandma could hear, that the way it concealed Sisi Bola's condition was certainly a triumph. At any rate when she arrived in the church, judging from the gasps of admiration, everyone appeared to think that Sisi Bola looked very well in her thirty yards of white silk brocade and lace.

Akin Ojo looked very well too in his morning coat and both of them made their responses nice and loud when Bishop Wilson-Harris made them man and wife. I must say it was a relief when it was all over and we were walking back down the aisle after signing the Register. I looked across at Mama and Grandma, and my brother, who waved at me. I remembered just in time not to wave back. At the reception, Mama pointed out to my father how well I'd behaved, but he only said that that was what he would have expected. However in case tiredness on our part should lead to a deterioration in our standards of behaviour, Grandma suggested that my brother and I, and the other two younger bridesmaids, be taken back to the house early for a rest before the second party in the evening, but not, she said, before the speeches were made and the telegrams read out and we'd had a taste of the six-tiered wedding cake.

I was happy to get back. I wanted to talk to Yowande, whom I hadn't seen all day because of being a bridesmaid, to ask her if it was true that Yetunde was sick. I overheard Alaba telling Patience this morning that she'd been taken ill in the night.

Yowande was not in the street where I had expected to find her. Our street was closed off for the night, tables and chairs had been set out there as well as in the courtyard and you could have heard the music I should think from five miles away. I was dancing with Tunji because Mama said it was my duty to look after him. We were showered with money for our dancing, Tunji delightedly snatched it from our foreheads as soon as the people sitting at the tables put it there, but it was for my dancing really. I dragged him with me into the courtyard which was as bright as day, but I couldn't just leave him, so I looked around for the Foster pink and spotted Aunt Rose dancing by herself on the edge of the crowd.

'Aunt Rose,' I called, pulling Tunji with me, 'look, I have a partner for you.'

I left him with Aunt Rose but I was afraid he'd lose the money so I took it from him. It was Aunt Rose who said I'd give it back later, not me. As I ran off quickly I wondered how much money Yowande had made. I found her at the top of the steps leading into the conservatory. We pushed our way into the house and counted our money under the table in the dining room; she hadn't made as much as me.

Yetunde was sick, she said, it was true. I said we should go and tell Nimota but Yowande said she was going to carry on dancing.

I found Nimota out in the street dancing with Kemi. Her pink 'up and down' was very tight and her bottom stuck out like Table Mountain; you could balance a tea-tray on it, Patience said, but then she had no bottom at all.

'Nimota,' I said.

'What is it?'

'Bend down, I want to whisper in you ear.'

'Make it quick oh.'

'Yetunde is sick, the magic must be working.' I winked heavily and nodded my head in Kemi's direction, just in case she didn't understand.

'What did you say?' Kemi asked me.

I opened my mouth to tell him but Nimota clapped her hand across my face and dragged me away.

'Shut your mouth or I go beat you!'

I was surprised. 'I thought you'd be pleased,' I said.

'I don't want your help!' Then, seeing my face, she put her arm around me and pointed towards Patience. 'Look, go help Patience over there, dancing with Ade.'

'All right, I'll go and see if Patience wants anything.'

But when I approached her she wasn't pleased to see me either. Hey ho, perhaps Aunt Grace needed me. I picked up a piece of akara, took a bite and ran inside.

Grandpa did not come downstairs for the wedding celebrations. He laughed loudest when I told him about Nimota and her spell, but he frowned when I told him that Aunt Grace had danced all night with Uncle Bode. He should have come down, I told him, he would have enjoyed it.

'Grandma did, but she is exhausted now,' I said.

'Exhausted! That much enjoyment would have killed me.'

'Don't be silly, Grandpa.'

– Chapter 3 –

'I want to hear a story,' Tunji said.

'You will have to come over here,' my mother told him.

That was impossible because Tunji and I were marooned on an island in the middle of the Niger river and we couldn't swim across on account of the man-eating alligators. If we'd been in Lagos still the situation would have been simple, there would have been someone passing by to ferry us across, here we might have to wait for hours; my mother wanted to finish her sewing and Patience was nowhere to be seen.

Mama preferred it here in Enugu to Lagos: I heard her tell Patience, who said that was because Grandma wasn't here. My mother said that wasn't true, she liked it because her life was more modern, she was able to go to the Club and the swimming pool and see the latest films. Hmm, Patience said. I would have preferred to stay in Lagos, but my mother had insisted on my returning with her and my father after the wedding, because Grandpapa and Bigmama were due to visit and they had not seen me in a very long time. They were my grandparents too, she said.

'You could tell us a story from there,' I said.

'No,' my mother shook her head and threaded her needle again.

It was not like Lagos at all. For one thing there were very few people in the house: only my mother and father, my brother and me, oh, and my baby sister Aduke; there was Patience, of course, Baba Cook, Augustus, the small boy, Rafaella the nanny, Florence the maid, and Sam the gardener. And for another, my father kept lots of animals as pets; he had his own private zoo, my mother said, and nothing angered him more than seeing them ill treated. In fact when we arrived my father had actually threatened to beat Baba Cook because Boswell the Great Dane had been in such bad shape. When he heard the car the poor dog came out onto the veranda swaying as if he was drunk, unable to lift his head from the ground. He resembled a cartoon drawing of himself, his head and feet looked huge because the rest of him had grown so thin. My father rushed up to him and examined his eyes and opened his mouth and then he shouted for Baba Cook.

'Baba Cook!'

Baba Cook came running with the rest of the servants following behind.

'Yes, sah.'

'Look at the dog.'

'I look, sah.'

'Well?'

'De dog am not well, sah.'

'I can see that, what have you to say? You have not been feeding him as I told you.'

'Sah, I go feed dat dog day and night, I no go make am if he no want chop.'

'Make am,' said my father, 'make am! This dog is dying of hunger, his ribs are coming through his skin.'

It did seem possible that Boswell was going to expire on the spot. Even the baby could have seen that this was a tricky situation for Baba Cook. But then he had an inspiration; he said, 'Sah, I tink the dog miss his master,' and he looked to the other servants for confirmation. They all nodded vigorously.

'You think so?' my father said and, forgetting about Baba Cook, he sank down onto the steps cradling Boswell's head against his chest.

Baba Cook was no fool, Patience said afterwards. I don't think Grandma would have believed him, but, as my mother said, Papa really loved animals. She didn't know where this trait came from, and it caused him great pain because his pets mostly died. If the tsetse fly didn't get them, the servants did: as Patience said, animals were only good for food. I loved the animals, in this respect I was like my father, my mother said. They couldn't talk though and Boswell was not the same as Yowande.

My father strode into the room, 'What are you doing there?'

'We are waiting for a ferry,' we said.

'Where to?'

'To Mama over there.'

'To bed,' she said.

We reached a compromise: she would tell us a story in bed. Our house was a bungalow, like all the others on the Reservation. It was an appropriate name, my father said, because it was where the Europeans lived and they considered themselves an endangered species. It was one room deep and all the rooms had very dark highly polished floorboards and led into one another in a long continuous ribbon; each of them had doors and windows opening onto a wide veranda running all the way round the house: all of it was the Niger river; only the furniture was dry land, the rugs were floating islands and the curtains, the colour of old gold, were trees.

I wanted the Seven Dancing Princesses, Tunji wanted the Soldier and the Magic Tinder-box, Sleeping Beauty, I insisted, Hansel and Gretel he said. He liked the scary ones. Patience said, what about the story of Grandpapa and Bigmama. That was the story she liked best. It was Nimota's favourite too. We settled ourselves in the bed, Patience pulled down the mosquito net and my mother began.

'In a distant land known as the Gambia, in a blue house by the sea, there lived the son of a Merchant Prince: your grandfather. He lived alone with his three children – '

'Where was their mother?'

'She died when the children were very young.'

'What a shame oh!'

'The death of his young wife left him heartbroken, and in due course he decided to change his profession and go out and seek his fortune.'

There was no need to tell us his new profession; in our family Dick Whittington would have been not Lord Mayor but Lord Chief Justice.

'We know, we know, he went to England to become a Lawyer.'

After an uneventful sea crossing, my mother said, he landed safely in London and proceeded to have many interesting adventures.

'Tell, tell!'

'I have time for one only tonight,' she said. 'Shortly after your grandfather arrived in the capital, he decided to explore the East End, which was on the opposite side of the city from where he lived. After walking for an hour or two he realised he was completely lost so he knocked on the door of a nearby house and a woman opened the door. Upon seeing him, and before he could utter a single word, she started to scream very loudly. Frightened by the noise of her screams he hurried off back down the path as fast as his dignity would allow, while she, still screaming, disappeared into her house and slammed the door. The next day after some reflection and feeling braver, your grandfather dressed himself very carefully, returned to the same house and knocked on the door; recognising him, the woman apologised profusely.

'I'm so sorry, luv, but I thought you was the lunatic they said had escaped around here yesterday.'

'Was he a black man?' your grandfather asked, surprised.

'No, why should he be,' the woman replied, and then as the penny dropped, she exclaimed, 'O my goodness it couldn't have been you could it!'

My mother's hands flew up to her face in imitation of the woman's dismay. The woman's expression was so comical, my mother said, that my grandfather burst out laughing; and so did we, while Patience shook her head incredulously at yet another example of the unfathomable behaviour of English people. When our laughter had ceased, my mother continued.

'In spite of his adventures, your grandfather was lonely in London where he had no close friends. He was therefore delighted when a fellow student suggested they both go dancing at the Hammersmith Palais, a well-known place for dancing in London. Your grandfather loved ballroom dancing and it was on that very same night that he first saw the lovely Miss Pickering standing alone on the other side of the crowded dance floor. He asked her to dance, and there and then they fell in love under the spangled lights. When your grandfather's studies were over, without a backward glance she came away with him to Africa, leaving her nine brothers and sisters, and her job in the glove factory in Neasden.'

The lovely Miss Pickering, or Bigmama as we called her, had no children of her own. My mother said she brought up her husband's immaculately although, she said, they were shyer than birds to begin with and it took time to tame them to her hand.

Bigmama was old now; her white skin had crinkled like tissue paper, all the colour had leached from her eyes, which had once been a brilliant blue, my mother said. In stark contrast she had very black hair, which Grandma said she dyed, and scarlet painted lips. Yowande and I could see that she and Grandpapa must have been an arresting sight as they dipped and swirled beneath the lights, because Bigmama was five feet eleven inches in her stockings and Grandpapa was six feet and a half in his. But we heard Patience say to Nimota, mysteriously, that they stopped the traffic in London for quite another reason altogether. She wouldn't tell us what it was.

Patience was frantic. 'Come on now. Fast, fast. We dey go Lagos.'

'Why do we have to go to Lagos?' I asked. 'And look it's not morning.'

'Your mama will tell you. Go. Go. She dey wait for you.'

We hurried into my mother's room, walking on the boards, our game forgotten. She was sitting in a chair nursing the baby and directing the packing at the same time. The maids scurried between the cupboards and suitcases seemingly buried under an avalanche of clothes. My mother told us calmly and quietly that Grandpa had died and gone to heaven. We wouldn't see him again. It was hard to believe that Grandpa would have gone away for ever without telling me, his favourite, the eldest grandchild. I would see about this when we got to Lagos.

Impatient to be off, I rushed out dragging Tunji, pestering the driver for quite some time about the length and duration of the journey to Lagos before my father and mother hurried out. Patience scooped up my brother who had fallen asleep where I'd left him propped up on the veranda. Papa was still shouting as the doors slammed and the engine roared.

I must have fallen asleep because we were being shaken awake again. The car had broken down. There was nothing for it, my father said, but to decant onto the side of the road and flag down a lorry. He was surprisingly calm, but it was the calm of desperation. This delay represented a disaster of such magnitude that he was temporarily not himself. He was the eldest son, nothing could begin in Lagos until he arrived. Our driver had prudently disappeared.

We settled down for a long wait. When all hope was gone, a lorry raced past and crashed to a stop some way ahead. After lengthy negotiations, the driver backed up and helped put in the luggage. My mother and the baby, my brother, myself and Patience climbed in the back. My father climbed into the cab with the driver.

He said, 'I have asked the man to take us to Lagos, but if I don't keep an eye on him, who knows where he will drive us. Also, I can act as a safety precaution,' he finished enigmatically.

It was very hot in the back of the lorry, there were no windows. Narrow planks, their ends resting on the ledges which ran along either side, served as impromptu seats. My brother and I were perched like budgerigars high above the floor. We took it in turns to overbalance and land upside down on our heads every time the lorry swerved around a corner.

Above the thuds my father could be heard berating the driver – 'You had better drive slower, slower, you hear?' – as we approached the corner, and then 'O my God,' as we negotiated it.

Each time my brother and I fell down, Patience laboriously picked us up and set us back on our perch again. On the straight too my father had good advice for the driver. 'You are going too fast,' he said, 'you will kill us all. We are on our way to bury my father and I must be there in person, not as a corpse.'

Throughout, the driver took no notice of my father and the speed remained the same, until my father told him, 'If you do not drive more slowly, I will put you in prison. I am a magistrate.'

At that the driver put his foot down on the accelerator and the lorry hurtled forward, swinging wildly from side to side.

My mother, laughing, looked sideways at Patience and said, 'I hope the safety precaution will keep quiet now.'

We heard no more from my father, but Tunji and I kept on falling to the floor and my mother finally prevailed upon Patience to let us sleep there undisturbed.

We were woken abruptly by the noise, which was deafening. Peeping through a hole in the tarpaulin, all I could see were faces as the lorry forced a way through the people packing the street. We had arrived. Emerging unsteadily from the darkness of the lorry, and blinking in the bright light, my brother and I were overwhelmed and suddenly terrified before the solid wall of sound being built brick by brick in front of us by the hired mourners. Their ululating shrieks seemed torn from their throats and flew upwards almost visibly, making the air as thickly thronged as the ground. Crying now, we had to be carried into the house.

The crush was just as thick inside. People filled the corridors, were jammed into the rooms and lined the stairs. Every inch was disputed as we made our way to our final destination, the central sitting room on the first floor, Grandma's room.

She was enthroned in the middle of it on her rocking chair. There was space around her. She rocked backwards and forwards in a stately rhythm. Behind her, resplendent in their best robes and jewellery stood her close female relatives, in attendance, ready to fan her, dab her with cologne and offer refreshment. She was immaculate. Her black silk dress flowed over her without a crease and her white lace collar matched the dazzling aureole of her hair, parted and plaited around her head. Her mouth was contorted in a huge 'O', and she was wailing, yelling at the top of her voice, fit to burst. The whole of Lagos, and those from out of town who had already arrived, looked on in approval and appreciation. She looked good and she was putting on a great show.

'Mind you,' as Aunt Rose was heard to remark, 'dis just de beginning, make a shout louder than anyone becos de whole world know she no like am.'

It was true. Grandma was expected to keep up her lamentation very nearly continuously for however long it took the relatives and friends to assemble. I knew for a fact that she and Grandpa had never exchanged a single word in all the time I'd known them, and that was all my life. Her behaviour was extraordinary.

I kicked at Patience to let me down and went straight to my grandmother. I climbed onto her lap, sure of my welcome. She hugged me to her without breaking her rhythm or stopping her crying. I wriggled free of her arms and looked into her face; her eyes were completely dry. That was better. I leant against her comfortably, and we rocked backwards and forwards together, taking a good look around.

The room was packed. Guests were sitting on chairs arranged in rows on three sides of my grandmother. The huge double doors to the north and south were thrown open today and revealed the rooms beyond, also packed with people. They were crammed onto yet more chairs, and where they weren't on chairs they craned up from the floor, or stood pressed against the walls.

The crossdraughts from the open windows which usually cooled the house were stifled at source by the press of bodies, and the fans whirring at full speed and buzzing like huge bees made no impression on the humid air. The house was a furnace.

Day after day, a constant stream of sympathisers, come to offer their condolences and to join in the mourning, passed in front of my grandmother. They flowed through the rooms, taking it in shifts so that the cycle wasn't broken and the momentum maintained. Grandma would have to pace herself, Aunt Rose said.

Tunji and I were sublimely absorbed in everything that was happening. We relished to the full this complete departure from normality. Our mother and father and the rest of the family were fully preoccupied. It was the easiest thing in the world to evade Nimota and Alaba. If by chance they cornered us upstairs, we merely dived under the nearest agbada and they could not, without impropriety, peer under people's robes to see if we were underneath. When we were outside they had no hope at all, there were far too many places to hide.

The courtyard at the back of the house had been transformed so that everyone could be fed. Fires were lit and whole sheep were roasted over them. Huge cooking pots simmered and bubbled. Yowande and I sat unnoticed at night listening with Tunji to ghost stories and watching the smoke and steam make eerie patterns against the sky. We gorged ourselves on roast mutton, jolof rice, dôdo, akara cakes and moin moin, steamed in banana leaves. Wherever we went, people pinched our cheeks and patted our heads, nodding theirs sadly at our loss. Therefore we were rather taken aback when a woman we recognised, because she had been present for several days, stopped me on my way into the house and said, 'Hey pickin, pickin, who dey die?'

'Grandpa, of course,' I replied, leaving her none the wiser.

The day finally came when everyone who had to be there had arrived. That's to say all Grandpa's children – my father Simon and his sister, Aunt Harriet, who were the two children of the Fante princess, and Aunt Sylvia, Uncle George and Aunt Grace, the children of Grandma Loretta, and also Uncle Henry.

It was shortly after that that Tunji and I were banned from the drawing room. Every time we tried to join the queue of people shuffling past, we were somehow shunted aside. Biding our time we slipped in amongst the folds of a fat mama's robes. What we saw made sense at last of everything that had been taking place.

We were not often allowed in the drawing room, only for

special parties and to pose for family photographs. We were always posed, smiling or otherwise, against the background of the flowered wallpaper, with someone invariably leaning nonchalantly on the piano. Now, all the furniture was pushed back against the walls. The room was dark and cool, with the same family portraits staring down from the walls and decorating the top of the piano. In the centre was a huge bed and on the bed was Grandpa. His face looked exactly as usual except his eyes were shut. He was dressed in striped trousers and a black morning coat. His top hat was by his side. He did not wake up: we realised he must be dead. We pushed our way out and went straight to Grandma. I cried as if my heart would break and Tunji, who hardly knew Grandpa at all, cried in sympathy. Grandma rocked us to sleep in her arms.

We children were not allowed to join the long procession to Lagos Cathedral and then to the cemetery. My grandmother and my mother, who was pregnant, did not go either. It was cosy with just a few of us in the house for a short while and we gathered in the sitting room. My grandmother sat back in relief. Fanning herself and stretching her legs out in front of her, she flexed her feet round and round admiring her ankles in their silk stockings. My mother who had ventured out of her room sat nearby. 'You must be tired, Ma,' she said.

'I am, my dear, I'm exhausted.' We sat in companionable silence. Then Grandma said, 'Mrs Adewole doesn't look good. I think she has been in a decline ever since her husband died. She's younger than me but I think she'll go before me just the same.'

'I think so,' said my mother.

'I haven't seen the Rotimis, were they here?'

'Yes, Ma, they came with the Effiongs.'

'Ah.'

'That Davis girl is much improved since her marriage, how many children does she have now?'

'Two, or maybe it's three,' my mother replied.

'I tink it tree,' Aunt Rose interposed.

'Nobody asked you,' said my grandmother sharply, and

Aunt Rose resumed her tea drinking, her little finger crooked as she did so.

'I suppose they've picked the place clean,' my grandmother continued, her eye on Aunt Rose.

'Cook say haf de kitchen go,' Aunt Rose said with satisfaction. 'By the time it finish, you no go see knife, fork or spoon lef in de house.'

'I don't know how they do it,' said my mother, 'even the baby's bottles have disappeared.'

'A big occasion like dis one go bring out de experts,' Patience said.

A little later my grandmother took advantage of the break to sleep in her room and my mother took the opportunity to plait my hair. My brother escaped outside. Not for the first time, I thought how much better it was to be a boy.

It was well into the afternoon when the wailing and shouting and the beating of drums signalled the return of the mourners. Now the true mourning would begin; it was inconceivable that the widow and children and relatives be left alone and unsupported in their grief. The celebration of my grandfather's long life continued for another two weeks and during that time the family were helped to reconcile themselves to his death. Surrounded by friends and relatives, talking and reshaping him, he became real again and incorporated once more into our lives.

We children knew for a fact that he had come back, because the food that we put out for him in his room on the night of his burial had all been eaten when we went to check the next day.

Nevertheless when the last guest departed, the emptied house lay on the hot street like a skeleton picked clean, with the wind whistling through its bones and the spirit gone out of it. Yowande and I sat desolate, in the courtyard under the trees. What would happen to us now? Life would not be the same, for sure, now that Grandpa was no longer alive and responsible for us all, up on the top floor.

Bigmama, who liked to wear chiffon, fluttered up the stairs in green, kissed the air on either side of Grandma's face, and then, like a giant cabbage butterfly, alighted on the sofa on the other side of the room. She continued fluttering for several minutes, the material of her dress floating gently all around her until tea was brought in and she settled and was still. Once Bigmama was established, Grandpapa, who had been standing by attentively, left her on the sofa and crossed over to Grandma. He gripped her hands tightly in his own to express yet again his sorrow at her bereavement, released her, and left the room with my father saying they had business to attend to. The rest of us, Grandma, Mama, Aunt Rose and I, turned our attention back to Bigmama. My mother sat beside her and stroked her hand, Grandma fixed her with an inscrutable look and Aunt Rose and I stared unashamedly.

Whenever my stepgrandmother came up for discussion in the house, and I was half asleep as usual on Grandma's lap, Aunt Grace was the one who spoke up in support of her, she said how much she admired Bigmama and how brave she had been to leave all her relations in England to come and live in a foreign land. It was truly romantic, Aunt Grace would sigh, adopting an appropriate pose and twirling the ends of her hair around her fingers. Aunt Rose snorted at such a ridiculous notion, and remarked that Bigmama would have had to be even braver if Grandpapa had not decided to leave all his relations behind too in the Gambia to live in a foreign land. Nimota explained when asked that Aunt Rose meant that Bigmama would have been unacceptable to Grandpapa's family on account of her being a foreigner and white. You could be sure, she said, that if Bigmama had set foot in the Gambia, Grandpapa's female relatives would have made life so unpleasant for her that she would soon have returned home. It was a fact that Grandpapa had elected to set up practice in Nigeria when he returned and not in his own country, and it was also a fact, as Aunt Rose said, that Bigmama would not have lasted five minutes if she'd been married to Grandma's son. It was fortunate, I thought, that Bigmama and Grandpapa didn't live in Grandma's house but all by themselves in Jos, where the weather was clement and where Bigmama grew Christmas roses in the same faded colours as herself.

There was silence for a while after my father and Grandpapa had left the room, then Grandma addressed Bigmama: 'I am sorry you have not been well.'

'It was nothing serious,' Bigmama replied. 'I am quite better now.'

Grandma, who knew nothing about English understatement, could not believe her ears. Bigmama had not attended the funeral, yet if she had not been seriously ill she should have been there. Custom demanded it, only being on her own death bed could possibly have justified her absence. Even I knew that.

'Your illness was nothing serious?' said Grandma ominously. 'I see.' Aunt Rose, who was not an admirer of Bigmama's and who sensed trouble, leant forward to speak but my mother forestalled her.

'You were not well enough to travel, were you, Mama?'

'Oh, I could not possibly have travelled, I was unable to leave my bed.'

My mother glanced triumphantly at Aunt Rose.

'Aha, so your illness was serious,' Grandma persisted to Bigmama who reluctantly admitted, 'Well, I suppose so, I am going to have some tests done while I am in England.'

'Ah,' said Grandma, mollified; honour had been satisfied.

My mother was able to breathe freely again, the bell had sounded so to speak for the end of the round and Bigmama was still on her feet. Next Grandma turned to the subject of England. She was at present very interested in England because three of her children were there.

Uncle George, her son, had had to return there after the funeral was over to settle his affairs before returning home for good and his two sisters, Aunt Sylvia and Aunt Grace, had accompanied him, Aunt Sylvia to begin her medical course at Edinburgh and Aunt Grace to study art in London – no one in the family had ever studied art.

'What is this art?' Aunt Rose had wanted to know. And when nobody answered her she said that it was her opinion that Aunt Grace only wanted to study in London because Uncle Bode was there. Surprisingly, Grandma had let it pass.

Now, addressing Bigmama again, she proceeded to interrogate her, the London expert, about the precise regulations which obtained in a certain well-known Christian Association's hostel for young women in Bloomsbury, in which Aunt Grace just happened to be staying. This time Bigmama was alive to the situation. According to Mama, she reciprocated Aunt Grace's affection and she knew what she had to do to allay Grandma's suspicions. In fact her guess was no better than anyone else's on the rules currently in force at the Young Women's Christian Association, Aunt Rose said later, but, keeping her nerve, Bigmama confidently described a regime that made purdah seem lax by comparison. Satisfied, Grandma sat back in her chair. Aunt Rose, looking unaccountably disappointed, took up her teacup again and stirred its contents vigorously.

Bigmama had definitely won the second round. My mother caught my eye and called out, 'Remi, go and call your brother and tell him to come and say hello to Bigmama.'

Anxious not to miss round three, I hurried off to find him. I wondered as I ran why Bigmama and Grandpapa had come to visit. I decided the reason must be that we had missed them at Enugu, on account of the funeral.

Alaba came looking for me. She found me sprawled with the rest of the children under the mango trees. It was the one relatively peaceful part of the day, and our stomachs were full after eating lunch. Too much of my favourite crain crain soup had distended mine to the size of a football, and I could only lie comfortably on my side; in this position I was watching two of the boys playing a noisy game of ayo, slapping the counters down hard into the cradles scooped out of the board, and, from force of habit, listening intently to the gossip going on behind. Tunji, fast asleep of course, was laid out on his back beside me.

Alaba shouted, from the top of the stairs, 'Remi, your mother is calling you.'

Loath to move, I pretended not to hear her, and she was forced to come the whole way down into the courtyard to fetch me. On the way back, before she could start scolding, I quickly pulled a face which I knew would deflect her, 'Alaba, look, look, who am I?' I said, squinting down my nose while pulling down the corners of my mouth, and elongating my neck like a disgruntled camel.

'You are a wicked child,' she said, then added gleefully, 'It is Bigmama's maid, Amina, not so?'

'Yes,' I nodded, pleased with myself.

Alaba cast a quick glance around and, seeing no one there, could not resist going one better, and mimicking the maid's peculiar camel trot as well. I fell in beside her and we rocked and swayed in unison towards my mother's room, two ships of the desert any discerning trader would have bought on the spot for cash. Alaba and I could imitate anything, a grain of sand even, if we tried. Yowande couldn't.

It was dark inside the room, my mother was sitting by the window sewing, and the light slanting in through the half-open shutter stencilled her in gold. As I entered she put down her sewing and beckoned me over. I walked across on tiptoe in case the baby was asleep in her cot. My mother cupped my face in her hands and looked down at me for a long time without speaking. I was content to gaze back: her lips curved in and out seductively and I could see my reflection in her eyes which were heavily fringed lakes of calm water. We did not resemble each other, my eyes were small and my mouth was the kind you could put your head and shoulders in and look around, my father said, but we did have the same nose, short and straight to the point.

'Remi,' she said, 'you are going to England. Your father has found a very good school for you, and Bigmama will take you with her when she leaves.'

I was completely taken by surprise. Everyone went to England, I knew that, but not until they were grown up. At last, I said, 'Whose house will I stay in when I reach England, Mama?'

'You will stay with the other girls in the school, you will sleep there with your friends. You will be together all the time.'

'I do not have any friends in England.'

'But you will have, my dear, you will make friends very quickly, and remember, Aunt Sylvia and Aunt Grace are there, so you will not be alone.'

'I do not want to go to school in England, Mama, not now; I will go later. Soon.'

'I am afraid your father has made up his mind.' My mother was crying. I ran from her to Grandma and I saw that she knew.

'It is a great opportunity, Remi,' she said. She took me onto her lap and hugged me so tightly I could not breathe: or cry either.

Time moved very quickly, every day it seemed there was some new item to be purchased, an enormous trunk from the market, new dresses from the dressmaker, shoes, socks, hair ribbons. My head was quite turned by all the preparations and there were moments as I was trying on some of the new dresses when, being rather vain, as Patience sadly pointed out, I was actually excited by the prospect of going to England. And also, as Yowande said, as I was accompanying Bigmama, I would be able to see for myself the Hammersmith Palais, that well-known place for dancing. I would certainly write to her about it, I assured her.

But the news about England was not all good. Bigmama insisted that she buy me a raincoat which she said I would need to wear every day. Clearly, I said to Yowande, that must mean that the rainy season was all the year round in England. She agreed that it must be so and I was gloomy once again.

Kingsway Stores was the big department store on the Marina. You couldn't miss it. The name was painted across the front in big red letters on a yellow background and although I frequently passed by it when taking my walk with Nimota on the two-mile stretch bordering the lagoon, I had never been inside before. Bigmama said it was exactly the same as the shops in London with different sections for different items. Children's clothes were sold on the ground floor towards the back of the shop and to reach them we had to pass first through the food hall with all the imported food from England, such as lettuces and cucumbers, then through the household goods, electronic equipment and stationery. Behind the counters, lady assistants in smart blue and white check uniforms waited to serve.

Bigmama chose a raincoat for me which was made of stiff heavy rubber material and encased me all the way to the ground. Seeing my look of alarm, she assured me and the lady assistant, who was looking doubtful too, that I would soon grow into it. She said the same about the matching rain hat which rested on my nose completely obscuring my vision and made me feel like a tortoise in its house. Grandma must also have felt that the coat did me less than justice, because when I paraded it again for her at home, she cried, 'The child must have some jewellery.' Bigmama said she thought jewellery inappropriate for boarding school. 'Nonsense,' said Grandma.

It was decided, after some discussion, that a simple necklace with a matching bracelet and some earrings would be sufficient for everyday wear.

The day of departure rushed open-armed to meet us; friends and family came by every day bearing gifts to wish me well and console my mother and Grandma. Among them were my two special friends, Ebun and Derin, my fellow bridesmaids at Sisi Bola's wedding. We swore undying friendship. Yowande and I had no need to swear. Yowande said she felt sorry for me, but she also said that she wanted to come too.

Patience was inconsolable. The rag doll she was making me was regularly drenched with her tears as it took shape in her fingers, causing the colours to run.

'Why?' she asked. 'Why dey make am go? Small child like this never go England before, na big man and woman go.'

I waited but Grandma had no answer. The last straw for both of them was when Bigmama insisted that all my hair should be cut off.

'They will not be able to manage it at the school,' she told my mother. 'They will not know what to do with African hair.'

46

'These people must be very stupid,' Grandma said, 'what is the matter with them? Hair is hair.'

'I know,' said Bigmama, 'but they are not used to it.'

'I am sure you are right,' my mother said. 'Unless it is properly oiled they will not be able to pass a comb through, and it will hurt her terribly. Patience, fetch the scissors, please. No, on second thoughts, Remi, come with me.'

Mama took my hand and led me off to her room and Patience followed behind. In half an hour my mother had trimmed my hair into a neat acorn cap which fitted snugly round my head.

'You look very nice,' she said when she had finished. Patience held up a mirror for me to see the back.

I didn't think so. I thought it made me look like a baby again and I said so.

'Not at all,' Patience said. But I did not believe her.

'That is much more suitable for school,' Bigmama said when we went back into the sitting room once more. Grandma said nothing and folded her lips tightly together.

A whole procession accompanied Bigmama and me to the boat the next day. Grandma and Grandpapa, my mother and father, and my brother Tunji, Aunt Rose, Uncle Henry, and Aunt Harriet, and my nurse Patience; I had said goodbye to Yowande at home. The passenger ship *Ariel* glistened in the sunshine, her sleek steel flanks curved up from the dock seemingly touching the sky, and on the long walk up the gangway, we kept our eyes firmly on the clouds for fear of looking down. Aunt Rose had to be helped every step of the way. Uncle Henry held her hand in front, and Aunt Harriet pushed her from behind. She was a wreck by the time she reached the cabin, and was loudly dreading the return journey down. Grandma, already ensconced in an armchair, told her to stop making a fool of herself.

As soon as the luggage arrived, Patience and my mother busied themselves making our two rooms a home from home. My dolls appeared by magic on my bed, my dresses sprang up like flowers in the wardrobe, and my favourite books lined themselves up, immediately accustomed, on the shelves. As for Tunji and I, we dashed around the ship laughing and shouting; now downstairs trying out the beds which we discovered ruefully had no bounce; now upstairs where my father and grandpapa were checking us in and seeing to the paper work. Uncle Henry whisked us up on deck, dangled us over the side and scared us, roaring and shrieking, half to death. There were people everywhere, flocks of birds wheeled overhead, and a breeze blew in from the sea. The siren sounded and my father declared it was time for all those not sailing to leave the ship. He swept everyone back up on deck, where Bigmama and I were promptly drowned in a monsoon of tears and kisses. Then we were waving, waving, waving. Our faces were still wet long after we had lost them from our sight.

After dinner we took a turn around the deck. It was dark now, the stars were spilled like paint across the sky, and the moon trailed a silver snail track along the sea. We were in the middle of nowhere. Suddenly I began to cry; I yelled so loudly I set the whole ship in an uproar. My step-grandmother was appalled, she tried to quieten me, first with sweets, which I threw overboard, and then with threats. I was beyond solace, it had not occurred to me until this moment that when we set off in the morning I would not be home again in the evening. I was six years old.

– Chapter 4 –

I did not at first remember where I was until reminded by the unfamiliar motion and the sound of seagulls. Kneeling up on my bed I peered dejectedly out of the window and was shocked by what I saw. This limitless expanse bore little relation to the waves which rippled and sometimes pounded on to the beach at home. Watery valleys stretched as far as I could see, green slopes rose and fell and sparkled in the sunlight; when I looked down, mysterious caves opened up and dropped away below. I felt impelled to take a closer look and, barefoot in my long white nightdress, I raced from the cabin to hang head down from the railings, my feet hooked precariously under a bar and my gown billowing out around me. The wind sang in my ears and the water rushing past made my head swim. I was lost for a time in wonder.

An insistent tugging at the hem of my nightdress brought me back abruptly. Swinging upright, I looked enquiringly over my shoulder: facing me was a living incarnation of my doll from England. Her unblinking blue gaze, bright pink cheeks and fluffy yellow hair were identical; the resemblance was so exact, I wondered whether she would say 'Mama' if you turned her over. She was the same size as me.

'Hallo.' I smiled, pleased at this unexpected playmate.

She did not smile back, she drew herself up even straighter and continued to look at me sternly, it was funny but her expression reminded me of Nimota.

'Why are you out here wearing only your nightie?'

She was also behaving like Nimota, which was peculiar in a child, I thought, even if she were English. Her appearance was odd too: her face I saw now was brightly painted and she was wearing uniform.

'My nurse wasn't here to dress me,' I said indignantly.

Suddenly she darted forward, seized my arm and began to march me along the deck like a prisoner.

'You are a disgrace,' she said. 'I'm taking you back to your cabin.'

There was no escaping from her grip, she was unexpectedly strong and had had the advantage of surprise. For once I was speechless.

In this fashion, joined awkwardly like Siamese twins, we arrived at the cabin. She relaxed her hold on me and I immediately wrenched myself free, taking refuge behind my step-grandmother. Bigmama had obviously been wondering where I was, and, to my further amazement, she greeted my captor by name.

'I found her half dressed and hanging from the railings,' Miss Smith said succinctly.

'My goodness!' Bigmama put her hand to her forehead.

'We cannot have her running naked all over the ship like a little savage. She will have to be kept in check.'

'No, no. I mean yes, yes.' Bigmama nodded distractedly.

Belatedly I realised that Miss Smith was not, as I had at first thought, an exotic child: she was a fake, no playmate, merely another tyrannical adult, albeit a tiny one. I rubbed ruefully at the spot on my arm where her small spiteful fingers had pinched me, feeling very aggrieved at being so taken in. Her chagrin was palpable, she did not have the look of someone who would easily forget or forgive my mistaking her for a child like myself.

Miss Smith suggested to Bigmama, who readily agreed, that we meet upstairs for breakfast in the ship's dining room in an hour.

Bigmama offered to help me into one of the new dresses my mother had made me for England, but I was obliged to help her instead, thrusting first my arms and then my head into the proper places. She was not an expert like Patience who dressed me at home. When Bigmama knelt to pull my petticoat straight, her face, level with mine, was covered with tiny hairs to which her powder clung, flouring her like a bun. Her arms and shoulders were spattered with freckles, and, I found, holding on to them as she fastened my shoes, furry to touch. Nothing was the same.

'Don't cry,' Bigmama said, 'you will see them all again very soon.'

Our toilette completed, she put on a large hat and swished out of the room, bobbing ahead of me with her toes turned in and bending her knees with every step. Alaba, my youngest nanny, could do her walk beautifully; I wished she were here with me now. I asked Bigmama how it was she knew Miss Smith and she said that Miss Smith was our special friend on the boat: she it was, apparently, who had helped remove me by force from the upper deck the night before when I had been overcome with homesickness.

'You were out of your senses,' Bigmama shuddered.

My recollection was imprecise, I remembered screaming a little bit.

'They must have heard you in Lagos! And already this morning, Miss Smith has saved you from falling overboard. We should both be very grateful to her.'

'I wouldn't have fallen, Bigmama, I promise you. Look, I had my feet hooked under here.' I showed her where on the rail. She grabbed hold of the top of the bar with both hands and leant against it as if she were about to faint.

'Spare me!' she said. 'I cannot bear to think of it.'

Bigmama was not a good traveller, you could tell, even though she had been on the sea many times before. She was forced to stop and steady herself against the railings twice more on our way to the ship's dining room. It was the movement of the deck, I suspected. The rocking of the boat affected me not at all; I ordered eggs, bacon, kidneys, mushrooms and tomatoes as soon as we had sat down, and when I had finished those I moved on to toast and marmalade. Bigmama looked on, eating nothing; I was clearly blessed, she said, with an iron constitution. Miss Smith on the opposite side of the table, pouring tea for her into one of the pretty flowered cups, agreed. Miss Smith must have had an iron constitution too, I thought, because she ate as much as me. I pointed this out to Bigmama.

After breakfast we transferred to a corner of the stateroom where Bigmama confided to Miss Smith that her doctors had recommended a long period of rest and recuperation and that this was the main purpose of her visit to England. She also told her that I was to be put into a boarding school, at which Miss Smith raised her thin pencilled eyebrows but said nothing. She confided in her turn that she was in the army, at which I raised *my* eyebrows. I could not help feeling sceptical about her usefulness as a fighter. Seated on a cushion on the bench seat, she looked to me more like Miss Muffet on her tuffet than a soldier for her feet were smaller than mine and her legs didn't even reach the floor. Catching my expression, she glared at me and big red blotches appeared on her face and neck. I watched with interest to see whether they would join up and turn her red all over.

'What is to be done about the child? She cannot be allowed to roam the ship unsupervised. If I may take the liberty of saying so, Mrs Thorne, in your present condition it is unlikely that you will be able to control her, and you will almost certainly have a relapse if you try.'

Bigmama looked at me as if trying to gauge how much trouble I was capable of. I put on my best imitation of an angel; Patience would have been proud of me.

'See how she has behaved already.' Miss Smith erased the image at a stroke, supplanting it with a picture of me lying on my back on the deck, clinging to the rail with both hands, drumming my heels on the floor and demanding with the full power of my lungs that the ship be turned back to Lagos. Bigmama and I looked at each other, remembering.

'I really do not know what to do for the best.'

'Why do you not leave her to me? I could take her through her lessons in the morning and make sure she has plenty of fresh air and exercise in the afternoon. Get her in trim for school.'

With Bigmama's permission, Miss Smith continued. She

would be happy to draw up a programme for my instruction and containment. Bigmama declared that she would be extremely grateful provided that this caused Miss Smith no inconvenience. Miss Smith smiled the smallest smile I had ever seen. We could start straight away, she said. Dismayed I appealed to Bigmama, who relented. 'Not yet, in a day or two,' she replied.

I missed everyone: Grandma, Patience and Yowande most of all. It was lonely in my bed at night: that was when I cried. I would have cried all day too but Bigmama, who spent her time resting on her bed with the curtains drawn, assured me I would see them all again very soon. There were no other children on board and Bigmama did not like to talk, so lessons seemed not such a bad idea after all.

'Do not run like that, walk properly,' Miss Smith admonished me as I scampered along in front of her. She herself was teetering on very high heels, which made her taller than me. Ignoring the curious glances of the other people in the stateroom, she selected an unoccupied corner, motioned me into a seat and spread out the books she had selected from the ship's small library on the table between us. She remained standing. I watched her warily from my seat beneath the porthole while the sun struck sparks from her golden hair and glinted on the buttons of her uniform.

She selected a book, opened it at random and placed it in front of me. 'Can you read a little?'

'No.' I shook my head.

'No? How old are you?'

'I am six and I can read a lot,' I said, laughing.

The lady at the next table laughed too, but Miss Smith didn't. She was not amused at all.

'You will find that English girls are very advanced in their lessons, you will have difficulty, I imagine, keeping up with them.'

'Will they be cleverer than the girls at the CMS school?' I asked incredulously.

Sadly, I would not now be joining Yowande or my other friends there this term.

'Much cleverer,' Miss Smith said emphatically.

'Have you been there?'

'Of course, that's where I come from.'

'No, not England, to the CMS school.'

'I can't say that I have.'

Then how did she know, I wondered.

After the first few lessons I no longer wondered, I knew: Miss Smith was mistaken about English girls if these were the kind of tasks they were set. They were so easy, a baby could have done them. I tried to explain to her that I was much cleverer than that, everybody said so. Miss Smith did not believe me, she said it was not possible and continued as before. There was something the matter with Miss Smith. Grandma could have told her, I expect, but Grandma wasn't here.

'Bigmama, I do not want to have any more lessons with that woman,' I said, 'I want to stay here with you.'

'Perhaps tomorrow,' Bigmama replied, 'I don't feel quite myself today . . . It is very good of Miss Smith to take such trouble with you. Come here, let me button your dress.'

Reluctantly I crossed the cabin to where Bigmama lay on her bed, draped in the long folds of her pink satin négligé. She turned me around so that my back was towards her, fastened the buttons on the back of my dress, and tied my belt in a bow. 'Miss Smith should be here at any moment to collect you. Brush your hair.'

There was a knock at the door and the crimped features of Miss Smith appeared around it. She said good morning to Bigmama and asked me if I were ready. Bigmama answered in the affirmative and the two of us departed, first to take breakfast in the dining saloon and then to begin our lessons for the day in the passenger lounge.

'Do not forget your books,' said Miss Smith as I ran out the door without them.

So far I had been confined almost exclusively to the company of Miss Smith, and the adventureless passenger lounge. But there must be at least a hundred different things to do on a boat, I calculated.

'I do not feel well,' I said to Miss Smith after lunch. Miss Smith looked at me suspiciously, but I opened my eyes wide and made myself go limp against the back of the yellow sofa, like Bigmama. Alaba my nurse would have laughed if she could have seen me.

'The poor child certainly does not look well,' said the woman opposite, who sat knitting every day. I opened my eyes at her too and slipped down sideways onto the seat. Miss Smith was forced to take me back to Bigmama.

'I will just lie here quietly on my bed, Bigmama, I won't disturb you,' I said. And I arranged myself on my pillow with my hand on my forehead, palm outwards just like Bigmama.

Miss Smith apologised to Bigmama for having to bring me back but she didn't see what else she could do. Bigmama's eyes were closed so she did not see the nasty look Miss Smith bestowed on me; Patience would have said that Miss Smith smelt a rat.

I emerged cautiously some time later, having genuinely fallen asleep, but there was no sign of Miss Smith lurking in the corridor or anyone else and I made it safely to the stairs. Instead of going up to the passenger deck where Miss Smith was sure to be, I went down the stairs to the third deck. The corridor there was also deserted. I began to tiptoe along, wondering where the doors led and looking mostly behind me to see if I were being followed, when a loud voice made me jump two feet into the air.

'What are you doing here, young lady?' it boomed.

The man in front of me was bright red and covered in hair which licked like tongues of flame out of the neck of his white shirt, up around his face in a beard and met in a conflagration on his head. Patience would have told me not to stare, but the fact of the matter was that Moses was less surprised than I when he beheld the burning bush.

'I am looking for my grandmother,' I said at last.

'Well,' the man said smiling, 'you won't find her down here. This is The Corridor, where the crew live.'

'What is the crew?' I asked.

'The crew are the men in charge of the ship, and I am in charge of them. I run the ship.'

'You are the Captain,' I said.

'No,' he said, 'I am the Bosun.'

'My grandmother is asleep,' I said.

'I see, so you decided to explore.'

Mr Lowther told me his name and asked me mine, he said there would be no harm in showing me around while my grandmother was asleep and I would not be missed. What would I like to see first? he asked. Everything, I said.

Mr Lowther said that the most interesting place was the main deck and we should start there. The floor of the main deck, unlike the wooden passenger deck, was made of metal and painted a reddish colour, and it would have been a huge open space except that every inch of it was filled. On the main deck, Mr Lowther said, space was money. We had to pick our way around enormous tree trunks which weighed several tons each, Mr Lowther said. They were individually lashed to the deck with metal chains on either side of the holds where the palm kernels and the cocoa beans were stored. You had to watch those logs if there were a storm in the Bay of Biscay, he said. This ship was a cargo boat. Fore and aft yellow painted derricks used for loading and unloading the cargo towered above the deck and suspended from their metal fingers were the canvas roofs of two huge tents which enclosed the space above the hatches of the holds. Inside the tents lived the Kroo. Ah the crew. No, Mr Lowther said, they were a tribe from Sierra Leone who were specially skilled at handling cargo and they carried out all the manual labour on the ship. I had seen them upstairs in the mornings on their knees polishing the decks and I had wondered where they lived, and now I knew. Bunkers filled the remaining spaces and Mr Lowther said that when we reached Las Palmas which was only six days out from England we would be taking on tomatoes and new potatoes and stands of bananas four feet high which would be ready for the market when we reached port. Except that there were no chickens on the main deck, I said to Mr Lowther, it was just like Jankara market on a Saturday.

The tour had taken rather longer than we thought and when we reached the passenger lounge in search of Bigmama, Miss

Smith flew to the door like an angry mosquito. I was a wicked and evil child, she said. Bigmama was in a dreadful state thinking I had fallen overboard. I had been quite safe with him, Mr Lowther assured Bigmama, and volunteered to take me around again the following day. It was better, was it not, he said, that I should be in responsible hands rather than risk my escaping again and wandering around on my own?

Miss Smith had swallowed her lips again. Yes, she agreed.

Nevertheless, Mr Lowther reassured Bigmama that he would instruct all the members of the crew to be on the lookout for me at all times.

'Thank you,' Bigmama said with a sigh and leant back against her chair. I went and sat next to her and stroked her hand.

'I was quite safe, Bigmama,' I said.

'Humph said Miss Smith.

After that Miss Smith could not keep me. Every morning I followed her meekly to the passenger lounge but when I asked loudly to be allowed to use the lavatory, making all the other occupants look up, she could not very well refuse. I did not return.

Miss Smith could not follow me onto the main deck and into the tents of the Kroo, neither could she go barging down The Corridor, and sit with the crew in their recreation room while they diced and played cards and told stories which I must admit I didn't understand. Nor could she follow me up onto the bridge where I went to take a turn at the wheel three or four times a day. Although she sighted me a hundred times a day she had no hope of catching me as Mr Lowther said the ship was made up of different worlds and only he and I could move freely between them.

After a week, Miss Smith told Bigmama she was giving up the unequal struggle, but I should not have looked so smug because a few days later fate intervened on her behalf. Mr Lowther had arranged for a swing to be rigged up for me on the passenger deck, and I was in the habit of using it in the afternoons after lunch when I knew that most of the passengers, including Bigmama, were taking their siesta. If Miss

Smith, who never took a siesta, should chance along, as had happened once or twice, there was a linen locker handy, into which I could disappear as if by magic. On this particular afternoon, I had taken lunch with Mr Lowther in the Petty Officers' dining room and had come upstairs rather later than usual for my swing. I had decided to see how high I could swing and I was at the top of the arc well above the railings when I recognised Miss Smith's wire-thin voice approaching. In my haste to rush and hide in the linen locker before she should turn the corner, I fell off the bar of the swing in time for Bigmama, who was taking an unaccustomed walk in the fresh air with Miss Smith, to see me skidding down the deck towards the railings, head first. The sight gave Bigmama such a turn, Miss Smith said afterwards, that she nearly passed away. And so for the next few days with Bigmama in attendance I was given up to Miss Smith again.

However I was not unduly worried. It would not be for long as we had passed Las Palmas days ago and any time now we would be arriving in Liverpool. I knew, you see, that my mother would be there, Grandma would be there, and my nurse Patience. Everyone waiting and waving. That was why, as I told Mr Lowther, I had not been very homesick on this journey. Is that so, Mr Lowther said. It was cold now and Mr Lowther and the rest of the crew had changed from their white shorts and white shirts and long white socks, into smart blue cold-weather uniforms. I wore my rubber raincoat and matching rain hat which Bigmama had bought for me at the Kingsway Store in Lagos every time I went on deck, and still I was cold. I said as much to Bigmama. Miss Smith, who was sitting with her, looked at me with a glint in her eye and said I would feel colder yet, colder than I could possibly imagine. She seemed pleased at the prospect.

'Land, look it's land.' Everyone was very excited, even Bigmama came out for a glimpse. I was in a frenzy, I could not really see anything, but I hurtled backwards and forwards all the same shouting 'land, land' at the top of my voice. Soon I would see them all. Liverpool was very dark. Even though it was day the sky was black and overcast and the water leaden.

On either side the buildings hugging the shore slid by in an endless grey ribbon as our ship sailed up the Mersey, through the Brunswick entrance and into Toxteth Dock.

There were people waiting on the quayside, looking up and waving. There was no one that I knew.

'Bigmama,' I said, 'where are they?'

'Who?' said Bigmama.

'Mama,' I said, 'and Grandma and Patience.'

'They are at home,' she said. 'How could they be here? This is England.'

I burst into tears, an unstoppable river of tears, which flowed down the front of my rubber raincoat, beneath my matching hat.

– Chapter 5 –

'It's not so bad.' Bigmama leant across from her seat and lifted up the brim of my rain hat so that she could look into my face. 'You'll see. You have uncles and aunts in England too, you know, don't forget I have nine brothers and sisters over here, they will love you just as much. And then there's Aunt Sylvia and Aunt Grace, they will both be eager to see you again. You will soon make new friends and in no time at all England will be just like home.'

I stared back at her silently; piqued, she released her hold and the hat snapped down again over my face like a visor so that no part of me was visible to the outside world: I had retreated entirely within my coat. I was indeed as Aunt Rose had foreseen in Lagos, like a tortoise inside its house. I was not crying any more, there were no tears left, I had cried them all last night at the hotel in Liverpool when I finally understood that Bigmama had lied to me and that Grandma, Patience, Mama and Yowande would not be coming to meet us after all. She said they would be coming to England very soon. I didn't believe her now. It wouldn't surprise me if I never saw them again. Hunched opposite Bigmama in my corner by the window, I looked out through the narrow gap between my hat and upturned collar and marvelled soundlessly at the shining ribbons of the railway tracks and the English countryside speeding by. We were on the train to London.

In England you could see right across to the horizon, the land was all laid out before you, tamed and tidy: dapper little forests, small neat fields surrounded by trim hedges and walls, a series of packages gift-wrapped and tied up with string. In the car, on visits to Mama and Papa out of Lagos, visibility was restricted to a few yards on either side of the road and the only signs of habitation were the blood-red earth tracks, leading into the heart of the forest. I preferred that: entering the forest you never knew what you might find, the villages were secret and mysterious, stopping was always an adventure.

'Knock, knock, can you hear me in there?'

I made no reply.

'Never mind, I know you're in there and I want you to listen carefully to what I have to say.' There was a pause and the sound of Bigmama clearing her throat. 'Remi?' I remained silent. 'I want you to stop calling me Bigmama,' she said.

I turned abruptly from the window and lifted my hat a fraction to look at her. 'Why, Bigmama?'

Her face was changed in England, more colourful, the pink in her skin and the blue in her eyes, sapped by the sun in Africa, were restored by the cold; paradoxically, she seemed warmed up.

'Well, because things are different here.'

'Why?'

'When you call me Bigmama, it attracts attention, people think it odd. After all I am not your real grandmother. It would be better if you called me Aunty.'

'If Grandma came to England, would I have to call her Aunty too?'

'No.'

'Why not?'

'That is not the same,' Bigmama said; her cheeks were very pink now. 'You and she, well, you and she are both African: you are the same colour. People here will find it very odd that I should be your grandmother, because you are black and I am white. I don't want any more questions, you will just have to take my word for it. From now on I want you to call me Aunty.'

'Yes . . . BigmamAunty.'

'Be very careful, Remi.'

'Yes, Aunty.'

Letting my hat fall back I swivelled around to the window again. Why were things different here? We were both the same colour as before, weren't we? Also there must be something wrong with Bigmama's eyes – Grandma and I were not the same colour, Grandma's skin was yellow-brown, I was more copper, like my mother. If only Grandma were here, I thought she would know.

Aunty Madge, Bigmama's sister, and her husband, Uncle Reg, met us at Euston Station. I liked them both immediately. Uncle Reg knelt down in front of me on the platform, swept off his hat, placed it over his heart and said, 'Very pleased to meet you.' His hair, slicked down with hair cream, merged and separated across his scalp exactly like the railway tracks I had seen for the first time on the journey down from Liverpool, and I was fascinated too to see that he had no teeth. Aunty Madge, tied in the middle with a thin belt, reminded me of the pillows on Grandma's bed, plumped out and soft, heaped one on top of the other and frilled with the neat sausage rolls of her hair. She was Bigmama's elder sister, in fact she was the eldest in her family, just like me. We were staying at their house in Wilton Avenue which was very small, half a house, I thought, looking at it, but Bigmama said that was not so, it was semi-detached; well whatever it was, it was a doll's house. There was a front room with a bay window looking out onto the street, and a back room with a french window opening onto the garden; three bedrooms, a kitchen and a bathroom. I had explored it in a trice. And there were no servants. I went looking for them, expecting to find them housed in their quarters at the bottom of the garden, as obviously there was no room for them in the house. Bigmama said there were no servants in England any more because of the war and when I asked her who looked after Aunty Madge and Uncle Reg, I was shocked to hear that Aunty Madge did. Apparently Uncle Reg went to work every day and Aunty Madge looked after the house. I felt very sorry for Aunty Madge. I could not imagine Grandma or Mama 'looking after the house' and it was rather peculiar seeing Bigmama making beds and preparing breakfast. I could not get used to calling her Aunty either.

'There's so much to be done, before she goes to school, I simply do not know how we will manage to fit everything in,' Bigmama moaned. She sat close to the fire painting her nails a virulent shade of scarlet and admiring each one in turn in the light of the tall fringed standard lamp which stood behind her in the corner.

'Are you sure that colour's bright enough?' Uncle Reg raised his hands, pretending to shade his eyes.

He and I sat opposite Bigmama on the other side of the fireplace, next to Aunty Madge's china ducks flying in formation up the wall towards the picture rail. Uncle Reg was teaching me to make roll-up cigarettes in the mechanical roller in the top of his tobacco tin. When he rolled one it worked like magic, his were uniform and elegant, mine resembled small bales of hay, badly packed, he said. Aunty Madge said I would see plenty of hay out in the country where I was going. She was sitting up at the dining table with her steel curlers in place, playing patience.

'I could go to school here in Neasden,' I said. There was a silence.

'Hey! Look at this!' Uncle Reg applied a match to the end of one of my roll-ups and dragged deeply. He immediately began to cough, doubling over in his chair spluttering violently. I thought I had killed him.

'It's all right,' Aunty Madge said, seeing my consternation, 'he hasn't got his teeth in, bang him on the back.'

I quickly did as she said and when he'd recovered she told me that she only allowed Uncle Reg to wear his teeth for meals and special occasions, because she was afraid that when he had one of his fits as he had just now, he would either swallow them and choke himself or cough them out and smash them.

We were cosy and comfortable in the back room with the curtains drawn. I felt safe here.

'Why can't I go to school in Neasden? I could stay here,' I said.

Bigmama blew on her nails. 'You know very well that your father has already arranged a school for you.'

'Then I could stay here in the holidays.'

'That won't be possible either, dear,' Aunty Madge said,

looking at Uncle Reg who was attempting valiantly again to draw on one of my cigarettes. 'We'd have you gladly, but it's his heart you see, the doctor says any excitement could kill him. We have to be very careful.'

It was a pity, I thought, that Uncle Reg's heart could not be removed like his teeth from time to time and given a rest, then I could have stayed with them.

'So where will I stay in the holidays?'

'You'll know soon, I promise, but first we have to buy you your school uniform.' Bigmama fastened the top of her nail varnish bottle.

Bigmama and I attracted a great deal of attention at the bus stop. On Neasden Broadway, on the three occasions I had been shopping with Aunty Madge, some people stopped short when they saw me and their mouths dropped open; you'd think they'd never seen a child before, I reported to Uncle Reg in the evening. Aunty Madge said that the impertinent remarks were unforgivable and no doubt inevitable, but she thought it might be a good idea all the same to discard my raincoat and hat, because frankly, the staring was not unconnected to my Lagos-style ensemble. Bigmama insisted, however; she was afraid I'd catch my death. Aunty Madge could have no idea, as she had never been there, of how hot it was in the tropics. 'That's as may be,' Aunty Madge replied, 'but I'm afraid that when this little one begins to make sense of some of the remarks, she'll catch worse than a cold.'

The woman next to me in the queue peered down at me in an interested fashion and looked friendly, I thought. So peering back at her from under my hat, I said, 'This is my first time in England, you know, and I have never been on a bus before.' She did not reply and I was just about to tell her again when Bigmama pointed out that the bus was coming. I raced up the stairs straight to the front and sat feeling giddy at finding myself up so high on a level with the trees, which brushed against the windows, their branches covered in yellow leaves.

'Any more fares now,' the bus conductor said. His cap was

nearly as big as mine but he had pushed his to the back of his head.

'Harrods, one and a half, please.'

'Where's the little 'un sprung from then?' The bus conductor asked the question which was hanging in the air. Everyone looked expectantly at Bigmama, including me.

'Africa,' she said.

'Is it a boy or a girl?'

'I am a girl,' I said, offended.

'Well I never!' said the woman sitting immediately behind us.

Interested, I turned to ask her what she meant, but Bigmama said very sharply, 'Remi, sit still.' And, reluctantly, I obeyed.

'Any more fares now, any more fares.' Shaking his bag like a wild thing, the conductor moved away down the bus, I glued myself to the window again and Bigmama noted where the bombs had dropped.

We were both extremely nervous when we left the lift on the school uniform floor. Bigmama had said that Harrods was like Kingsway Stores at home, but it was not true. This shop had six floors and from outside seemed bigger than Lagos Cathedral; it was all lit up at night, Bigmama said. That I could believe! It took us ten minutes to find the lifts but not before we had been redirected by a very unfriendly gentleman in the men's department, where Bigmama had taken us by accident.

I knew Patience would have said, 'No mind am,' but it was not so easy. We stood quite still to take our bearings, the whole floor was hushed and silent like a desert, and equally empty. And then across the miles of sand-coloured carpet, out of the purple shadows, as in a mirage, a figure dressed all in black hove slowly into view.

'May I help you?' she said in funereal tones, fingering the tape measure around her neck.

'Yes,' replied Bigmama faintly, although she towered above her. 'I require a school uniform for my, er . . .'

'Yes?' the figure said, looking down at me.

' . . . for this . . . child,' finished Bigmama.

'What is the name of the school?'

'It is Chilcott Manor School.'

'Will you kindly follow me, please?'

We followed her to a secluded corner where Bigmama sank gratefully into the chair placed for her, and I silently retreated inside my coat until nothing could be seen of me. Loftily the figure paced away to find the list and order tea. She returned all too soon and said, 'I think you might remove your coat.'

I did not move.

'Remi,' said Bigmama, 'take off your coat.'

I was incapable of moving.

'Tut tut,' said the figure, 'come now.'

Bigmama was forced to leave her chair and prise me, reluctant as any oyster, from my shell. There was a slight gasp from the saleswoman and we all stared at my reflection in the looking-glass. I was a frog on stilts, pink medallions decorated my arms and legs where I had scratched the skin from my bites, and already in the crisp English air my skin had become dry and grey and flaky. My hair no longer resembled a snug-fitting velvet cap; unoiled, it looked as if it had been hurriedly knitted onto my head with many dropped stitches where my scalp showed through.

'How old is she?' This was addressed to Bigmama.

'I am six,' I said.

'She is very tall, is she not?' Addressing no one in particular, she lassoed me with the tape measure.

Even Bigmama was shocked by the mountain of clothes requisite for a modern schoolgirl at the start of her career, and she adopted the same principle in selecting each item as she had when buying my raincoat in Lagos, that it should last me the rest of my life. Were I to become a giantess, and grow even taller than Bigmama, I could never hope to grow into the overcoat now enveloping me like a flood, and nothing could convince me that schoolgirls in England wore their tunics ankle-length.

Finally I stood uncomfortably twitching, draped from head to foot in new and unaccustomed garments as unfamiliar as their names: lisle stockings, woollen vest, liberty bodice, bloomers 'nigger brown' the saleswoman sang out, and ticked the item off on the list. Underknickers, shirt, tunic nigger brown, and finally, overcoat and velour hat, also in nigger brown.

'There,' she said triumphantly, 'it is done.'

She turned me around, and once again the three of us surveyed my image in the looking-glass. I burst out crying, great racking sobs shook me to the ground where I lay watering the sable carpet with my tears, while Bigmama and the saleswoman looked on helplessly.

Bigmama told Aunty Madge, over a cup of tea, on our return, that she'd been very much afraid when I fell down on the ground in the shop that she had been about to witness a repeat of my behaviour on the boat. She did not think she could have coped, she said.

'Poor little thing, what was the matter?' Aunty Madge asked, putting her arms around me.

'I don't know,' I said, 'I was afraid.'

'It shouldn't be allowed.' Aunty Madge rocked me in her lap just like Grandma. 'Why are they sending her away to school at her age?'

Stirring her tea and looking across the table very seriously at us both, Bigmama said, 'Remi's family, along with other families like hers in Nigeria, believe that it's imperative for their children to receive an English education, so that when the time comes and their country is given independence they will be ready and prepared: they are the ones who will be running things in the not too distant future. That's what her father told me. Over there you know they value education above everything.'

'I still say there would have been plenty of time when she was a year or two older.'

'Well, you may be right, Madge, but I know Simon thinks you can't start the education process too early, *and* that his daughter will come to no harm in England because she has family here: us. He takes it for granted that we will care for her like one of our own (naturally I assured him that we would) in the same way that they do in Africa. So he felt that my coming over at this time was an excellent opportunity to set her feet on the path, so to speak. They all think Remi is very fortunate.'

'Hmm,' Aunty Madge sniffed, hugging me closer in her arms, 'I hope they won't all live to regret it.'

'I sincerely hope not, I've given my word that they can rely on us . . . well, on you. I shall be in Africa, of course.'

'Of course,' Aunty Madge said. Bigmama gave her a straight look, and she continued, 'I mean of course we'll do our best. Mind you,' she lowered her voice so that I had to strain to catch her words, '*I* would not have chosen Betty, as you know.'

'But she is married to Theo, Madge, and that's important to Simon because *Theo is the head of the family*,' Bigmama said loudly back.

'So?'

'In Africa,' Bigmama nodded significantly in my direction, 'that is best.'

'Hmm.' Aunty Madge sniffed again.

The houses in the terrace where Uncle Theo and Aunty Betty lived were parcelled up, just like the fields, but in grey; each one with a little fence around a minuscule front garden. There were no trees.

Bigmama rang the doorbell and removed my hat in one smooth movement; the door opened, only a fraction at first, then very wide to accommodate Aunty Betty, who quickly ushered us in. Bigmama tried to embrace her, they had after all not met for over ten years, but Aunty Betty drew back with an expression of extreme distaste on her face, extricated herself as quickly as she could, and led the way to the sitting room at the back of the house. Being cube-shaped, she moved as if she really needed a leg on each corner but had to make do with two. I could not imagine what would happen if she had to go anywhere in a hurry. Bigmama sank thankfully into a chair. Aunty Betty paid no further attention to her but followed me to the fire where she relieved me of my rubber house; we stared at each other, unblinking, before she bustled out to make the tea.

Bigmama seemed anxious, continuously dabbing at her forehead and upper lip as if she were hot, whereas in fact it was rather chilly I thought; I rubbed my arms in their thin cotton sleeves to keep the circulation going now I was no longer wearing my coat. The fire in the grate looked, rather than felt, warm.

'Come here,' Bigmama said, stretching out her hand to me. I took it and sat on her knee while she straightened first my dress, and then my socks which had fallen down. Her hands fluttered all over me as I leant back against her, tweaking and patting and pulling. At last she said, 'I hope you are going to be good today.'

'Uh huh.' I was noncommittal, and wondered why especially today.

'If you are good,' she continued, 'Aunty Betty and Uncle Theo will look after you during the school holidays and be your guardians. They are used to children, they have two of their own, Gerald and Maureen.'

'Where are they?' I was interested.

'I think they must be at school, they are older than you.'

'How old?'

'I am not sure; Gerald is twelve, perhaps, and Maureen must be sixteen or seventeen.'

They were not children, they were virtually the same age as Nimota and Alaba. I was disappointed.

The door opened noisily and Aunty Betty shouldered her way back into the room preceded by a very large tray piled high with cakes and sandwiches. It was not until she had turned around to set the tray down on the table, that we noticed Uncle Theo peering apologetically at us from around Aunty Betty's enormous behind. Bigmama swept me off her knee, unfurled her five feet eleven inches from the chair and, draperies flying, bore down upon him like a galleon, pulled him into the middle of the room and kissed him soundly.

'Theo,' she exclaimed, 'it has been such a long time.' And she wiped her eyes with her handkerchief, completely overcome.

Aunty Betty, foursquare by the table, and I, warming my

legs by the fire, stood by observing the show; it was quite like home. Uncle Theo was much smaller than his wife and sister. He had a habit when feeling emotional – he was doing it now – of pushing back his cap and scratching his head, which was completely hairless.

'It fell out,' Aunty Betty said, when she caught me looking. 'He was in an accident and it all fell out.'

I assumed, correctly, that she was referring to his hair, and tried, without success, to look at something else. I found Uncle Theo very appealing. At home people were not hairy as a rule, it was something I was used to; the same could not be said of his lashless green eyes, or the little green teeth he revealed when he smiled.

The sitting room, already crowded with furniture, was now crowded with people too, and we all sat down again. Bigmama arranged her trailing skirts gracefully in the large armchair on one side of the fire, and Uncle Theo practically disappeared into the one on the other side, having been told to sit in it by Aunty Betty. She presided over the teapot from a straight-backed chair by the table, I sat on a stool in between Aunty Betty and Bigmama.

Aunty Betty's pastries were very good; I was just licking my fingers after my fourth, and entertaining thoughts about a fifth, when Bigmama complimented her on her baking. I nodded strenuously in agreement. Uncle Theo jumped up again. 'One last one,' he said placatingly to Aunty Betty, and passed me the plate.

'She has a healthy appetite at any rate, considering she is so skinny,' she said.

'No milk,' said Bigmama.

'No milk?' repeated Aunty Betty.

'Yes, on account of the tsetse fly.'

'I do not follow you,' said Aunty Betty.

'No cows,' said Uncle Theo.

'No cows?' repeated Aunty Betty.

'Because of the tsetse fly there are no cows in that part of the world, so there is no milk for the children . . . to build them up.'

'Ah,' she said

'Talking of building up,' said Bigmama, 'that is just what I wanted to talk to you about. Remi will need a place to stay in the holidays where she will be well looked after.'

Turning to look at me, Aunty Betty said, 'What are those on her arms and legs?'

'Sandfly bites,' I said, picking at one.

'Stop that,' Bigmama said, brushing my hand away.

'More flies,' said Aunty Betty. 'That place is full of flies I take it.'

'I did mention to Simon, her father, that as you already had children, you might be willing to take her in,' Bigmama said.

'I do not see why not,' said Uncle Theo, 'do you, Betty? It would be nice to have a little girl in the house again.'

Aunty Betty eyed the pastries and looked at me, also eyeing the pastries. 'There's still rationing, you know.'

'Of course her father would make sure you were not out of pocket,' Bigmama said hurriedly and, turning to me, 'Remi, you have not seen the garden, look there is a swing, go and have a swing.'

'It will be cold outside,' I said.

'No, it will not. You can put your coat on. Run along now.'

Uncle Theo opened the door for me and winked one of his pretty green eyes to make me feel better. I cannot say that it did. I listened at the door.

'She seems a nice little thing,' said Uncle Theo. 'She would not be any trouble, it is only for the holidays, Betty.'

'I don't know about that, she might be trouble. She won't be used to our ways will she, coming from Africa and all.'

'I can assure you, Betty,' said Bigmama, 'she is used to living in a very English way. I was the one who brought up her mother.'

'That's as maybe,' said Aunty Betty, 'but there's our good name to consider, what will it look like having a darkie kid in the house? I mean if people see me out with her they'll wonder whose she is . . . it might look bad. I wouldn't want any misunderstanding.'

'That is ridiculous, Betty, no one could possibly think she was yours.' Bigmama sounded rather cross.

'You'd be surprised what people could think round here. It's different for you, living in Africa, you'd soon change your tune if you lived over here.'

Aunty Betty's voice had become very loud and I decided I had better move into the garden, even though they had probably forgotten about me. To reach it I had to pass through the kitchen which was even smaller than Aunty Madge's. I sat on the swing moving gently, backwards and forwards. I didn't notice the cold. I wondered if Aunty Betty and Uncle Theo would take me in the holidays; I hoped so as there did not seem to be anyone else who could have me.

I was not surprised at what I had heard because of the strange conversation with Bigmama on the train coming down from Liverpool. I still had no idea what it signified but I realised it must be part of the same thing. I dearly wished Grandma were here as there were two questions I wanted answered: what was a darkie, and what was rationing? Those were the things that seemed to be troubling Aunty Betty; if they could be put right there would be no reason for her to say no.

In the end, Bigmama and Uncle Theo won the day because by the time we left, Aunty Betty had agreed with Uncle Theo to be my guardian. I had hoped to meet Gerald and Maureen, but as Aunty Betty said, there would be plenty of time for that when I came to stay; Uncle Theo smiled at me conspiratorially, and pressed sixpence into my hand behind her back.

I cried when I said goodbye to Aunty Madge and Uncle Reg, my two best friends in England. Uncle Reg, like Uncle Theo, gave me sixpence instead of his tobacco tin which I coveted, and Aunty Madge gave me a boxing kangaroo wearing big red gloves. I clutched the kangaroo, my two sixpences, and the rag doll Patience made me very tightly in my lap as I sat next to Bigmama in the taxi taking us to Aunt Grace. Aunt Grace was studying art now in London and staying at the Christian Women's hostel. She would accompany me to school. I cried again when in the drawing room Bigmama shook out her skirts ready to leave and kissed me goodbye; I clung to her and wrapped my arms around her waist – she had been my only constant in the past few weeks.

Holding me away from her, she said, 'I shall not know what to do with myself now, I shall miss you. Be good, we are all expecting great things of you, Remi, and I know you will not let us down.'

'No,' I said, and waved her tearfully down the street. I felt as if I were on the boat again, it seemed that my life since then had been one long goodbye.

'I have cooked some rice,' Aunt Grace said, 'and fried some chicken. I even have some dôdo, your favourite. Come up now and meet my friends, they are expecting you. It is always a special occasion you know when someone arrives from home. You can tell us the news while we eat.'

Fried chicken and rice, happiness, sheer delight; we took the stairs two at a time and burst into the room she shared with two other friends from home. There were clothes strewn every-where among the tall stacks of crazily leaning books which took up much of the available floor space; a gramophone gaped open-mouthed in the corner, a black swirl of records lapping at its feet, and an electric ring, bristling with still smouldering hot combs, shared the windowsill with jars of pomade, beauty aids, and magazines. There was no place to sit except on the beds where Aunt Grace's two friends lolled, sleek and satiny as seals.

'My God, look at that hair,' wailed one, wrinkling her small flat nose.

'And look at her skin, what have they done to her?' the other joined in on the same note of despair, her fine Asiatic eyes narrowed in genuine horror. Lunging for me simul-taneously, they caught hold of my legs and arms and pinned me down, and rubbed and oiled and buffed me until I gleamed like polished mahogany.

The room was cramped, noisy and warm and the singed cinnamon smell of recent hair pressing mingling with the scent of coconut oil and sandalwood took me back directly to the house on Bamgbose Street.

'OK, you've had your supper,' Aunt Grace snatched my

plate, licked clean, from my grasp, 'now you must sing for it. Tell us absolutely everything, without omitting a single detail, of what was happening in Lagos before you sailed.'

'I can't remember,' I said. I had eaten so much I wanted only to fall asleep.

'You had better remember oh!' Aunt Grace said, looking at the other two, 'otherwise we will make you. We have our methods.' They started towards me across the beds.

'Stop, stop. I remember!' I said. 'Let me see, first we had another wedding: you remember Cecily Cole? Well she married Olufemi Adegboyega; the marriage was in true Yoruba style. Aunt Rose said it was a proper wedding not like Sisi Bola's and Grandma said proper or not she was happy that Sisi Bola's nuptials had been a Christian occasion. It was good fun, I was with Grandma and Aunt Rose at the bride's house when the bridegroom's family brought the formal proposal, it was in a letter, you know, carried on a tray all decorated with ribbons and flowers. I couldn't understand why the bride didn't accept straight away, we all knew she was going to say yes but she had to wait for a whole month. It didn't do for a woman to seem eager, Aunt Rose said, but how would she know, she was never married, Nimota said. We had pounded yam at the bridegroom's house on introduction day, and the ewedu soup was delicious. Aunt Rose told Yowande and me that introduction day was for the families to get to know each other, but we all knew each other anyway. Grandma would not let me drink any palm wine and when she wasn't looking Aunt Delma let me have a sip of hers, it's sour.'

'O God, ewedu soup, I can't bear it! What colour was the asoebi?'

'Ours was green, Ebun Ogunsola's family wore blue and Derin McKenzie's was yellow, I think.'

'What else, what else?'

'When the time came for the bridegroom to claim the bride we all danced through the streets to the Calabar Drum Band from the bridegroom's house to Cecily's house, halfway across Lagos, and Tunji got lost. Patience found him again, she cried from the shock but he was laughing. Grandma said we should thank God he had come to no harm.'

'Oh for the sound of the Calabar Drum!' Aunt Grace swung her hips caressingly in a slow circle and executed a few impromptu steps. 'You will find, Remi, that no one dances over here. How is my mother?'

'She questioned Bigmama very closely about you.'

'What did she want to know?'

'She wanted to know the rules governing your hostel.'

'And what did Bigmama say?'

'She said that it would be easier for a young man to gain entry to the harem of the Sultan of Turkey than to penetrate your portals . . .'

'*My* portals! Are you sure she said that?'

'No, I remember now, it was "*those* portals". I think she meant Uncle Bode.'

All three fell backwards onto the beds laughing. Aunt Grace giggled so uncontrollably that her hair fell out of its pins and down over her face, temporarily obscuring the perfect arches of her eyebrows.

'How is Uncle Bode?' I asked, mystified.

'Still outside, I believe.' Aunt Grace's friend, still laughing, looked sideways at her.

'Will I be able to see him?'

'No, there won't be time before you go to school,' Aunt Grace said, 'but I promise you will see him when you come again to visit.'

The school my father had chosen was an Elizabethan manor set in a fold of the Sussex Downs, and on this first afternoon there were lights only in the central body of the building, the wings on either side were in darkness. Aunt Grace expressed surprise: 'Why are there no lights? We must be early, the other girls cannot have arrived yet.'

I was so frightened I could not speak. The house looked even bigger than the boat, besides which I was having a certain amount of difficulty climbing the stairs on account of the long trailing skirts of my gigantic overcoat and lack of visibility inside my matching nigger brown velour hat. I had exchanged one tortoise house for another.

We were greeted in the huge chilly drawing room by Miss Bowles, the headmistress, and Miss Valentine, the vice-headmistress, a maid having shown us in. They rose simultaneously from their chairs by the fire and came towards us through the gloom.

Miss Bowles, small and fair, had on a long dark skirt and moved as if on castors, Miss Valentine on the other hand strode forward on strong thick limbs like piano legs. The introductions over, we were drawn across to the fire and settled side by side on a deep red sofa facing the two ladies. Aunt Grace shivered and drew her fur, which she had sensibly refused to relinquish at the door, more closely around her. I very much hoped I would not be asked to remove my coat as it was distinctly chillier inside the house than it had been outside.

'Dreadful weather for the time of year,' murmured Miss Bowles.

Aunt Grace and I had never been in England at this time of year before, but we both nodded politely and Aunt Grace said feelingly, 'Yes, it is.'

'Will you take tea,' said Miss Bowles, making it a statement not a question, and rang the bell.

'Yes, please,' said Aunt Grace.

There was a pause while Aunt Grace turned her head and looked around the room, and then, with the long feather on her indescribably fashionable hat once more pointing at Miss Bowles, she exclaimed, 'It is very silent, where are all the other girls?'

Miss Valentine's baritone now boomed out, 'There are no other girls here. Term does not begin for another week. We were not expecting you. You have made a mistake.'

'I have not made a mistake,' said Aunt Grace, not in the least put down.

'There has been an error,' said Miss Bowles soothingly. 'We must now consider how we may rectify it. I – '

She was interrupted by the maid arriving with the tea tray

and I found myself juggling with a teacup and saucer, a napkin, a plate upon which there was an unidentifiable, soon to be flying, object and a fork. Mercifully Aunt Grace relieved me of the teacup, and I picked up the dry yellow rectangle from my plate and was raising it to my lips when Miss Valentine spoke again. 'I would suggest you use the cake fork provided.'

I hurriedly put the cake back onto the plate and, holding the cake fork like a trident, speared it through the heart, shattering it into a thousand tiny fragments which flew up into the air and landed in a shower all over the fine Turkey carpet.

'Ah ha,' said Aunt Grace with some satisfaction, 'it would have been better to let her eat by hand.'

Miss Valentine, throwing us both a look of pure malevolence, rose briskly from her chair, pulled angrily on the bell, and remained standing by the chimneypiece as if on guard.

Aunt Rose would have been very scathing of Miss Valentine. She had no bust and even less behind and appeared to have a board inserted down her back. Her cheekbones looked sharp enough to have sliced through rock and above them her hair rose up in petrified blue-grey waves. She disliked me, she told me later, the moment she saw me; I disliked her, though of course I told her no such thing, the moment after. It took me longer, however, to stop being afraid of her.

I turned away and looked instead at the maid, who under direction was brushing up each separate crumb – 'You have missed some, look over there, and here' – until not a single speck remained.

'I think,' said Miss Bowles, who had stayed wonderfully still throughout, her hands folded like ivory fans on her lap, 'you should meet Matron, I shall go and fetch her.' And she rolled smoothly and silently from the room.

Behind her the temperature dropped by a degree or two. Aunt Grace took hold of my hand and we moved closer for warmth; Miss Valentine, adamantine, stared straight ahead. Presently Miss Bowles returned accompanied by the almost preternaturally aptly named Matron Bacon, who tripped lightly across the carpet on dainty pink trotters and, crackling with starch in her white nurse's uniform, pulled up another chair to the fire. I stared in dismay at her little piggy eyes and upturned snout set off by her stiff white cap and I decided that I could not possibly stay with these people in this school.

It was a miracle sent from God that term had not yet begun, for I would have a week in which to convince Aunt Grace, who had now seen with her own eyes what kind of a place it was, and who in turn would convince my father that if I were forced to go to school in England, I would surely die. My father would not be pleased but even he would not want that. The whole idea could be forgotten and I could go back to Africa with Bigmama. So it was with huge relief that I heard Matron say, 'It is a pity you have come all this way only to have to turn back again.'

Aunt Grace dropped her bombshell.

'I cannot take Remi back with me, I am a student at college and there would be no one to take care of her during the day.'

'Is there no one else who could take her?' enquired Matron, 'no other relatives?'

'We do not have relatives in England,' said Aunt Grace.

'I could stay with Bigmama,' I said, panic rising.

'No, you cannot,' replied Aunt Grace. 'Bigmama has to go into hospital for medical tests and Aunt Sylvia is out of the question, she is in Edinburgh, too far away.'

There was a lengthy silence during which I held my breath. The three Englishwomen consulted in whispers among themselves while directing swift speculative glances at Aunt Grace and me waiting anxiously on the sofa opposite.

'Is there simply no one with whom the child can be left?' Miss Valentine enquired again, exasperation plain in her voice.

Aunt Grace struck the arm of the sofa with her open palm, causing the rest of us to blink. 'Emphatically, no!' she said.

After a pause, Miss Bowles said softly, 'I would suggest, in that case, there being no alternative, that she stay here.'

'Thank goodness, I would be at my wits' end otherwise. You are sure it will not be inconvenient?' Aunt Grace rose from the sofa, drawing the collar of her coat protectively around her chin.

Ignoring her, Miss Valentine said sternly, 'The girl will be in your care, Matron.'

'Very well,' said Matron, ushering us from the room.

'Don't leave me, Aunt Grace, please don't go,' I cried, my fingers embedded in the fur of her coat, dragging her back.

'I have to go,' she said, 'believe me I would take you with me if I could but I cannot. You must be a brave girl, I shall come back to see you as soon as I can.'

'Don't go,' I wailed, 'don't go,' as Matron opened the front door.

'That is enough,' said Matron. 'You must say goodbye now or your aunt will miss her train. Do not worry,' she said, removing my fingers from Aunt Grace's coat, 'we will take good care of her.'

Aunt Grace ran down the steps and into the waiting taxi. I stood absolutely still at the top of the steps straining my ears for the last sound of the taxi as it disappeared down the drive. I was too desolate even to cry.

'We must go inside,' Matron said. 'We will catch our death out here,' and she pulled me inside and shut the door. 'Come, dry your eyes, blow your nose and you will soon feel better. Where is your handkerchief, is it in your pocket?'

I had taken off my hat when I arrived but I was still wearing my overcoat. 'Dear, dear,' she said, rummaging about in my pocket, 'we must have this off now.' And handing me my handkerchief, she began divesting me of the coat, which she put down on a nearby chair.

'Follow me,' she said, 'I have asked for your supper to be put out in the dining room.'

The dining room was another enormous room with dark panelling; our footsteps echoed on the polished wooden floor.

'For what we are about to receive, may the Lord make us truly thankful. Amen,' said Matron.

I unclasped my hands and opened my eyes. 'What is this?' I said.

'It is very nice, poached smoked haddock on toast.'

'What is haddock?'

'You do not know? It is fish, smoked.'

So far all English school food was yellow. On my plate half of a bright orange fish lay dry and stranded on top of a slice of toast which had drowned in the liquid that had been meant to sustain the fish.

I tasted it. 'I cannot eat this,' I said.

'What did you say?' asked Matron, her snout twitching.

'I cannot eat this,' I repeated.

'One of the rules of this school is that you must finish everything put before you. Try again.'

I put another portion in my mouth, but it was no good, it tasted disgusting. I put my knife and fork down; definitively.

'Very well,' said Matron, 'I shall let it pass on this occasion as it is your first day, but I assure you you will have to finish every single mouthful tomorrow.'

Hmm. We would see.

'Are you quite sure you do not want anything to eat?'

'I am quite sure.'

'In that case we might as well put you to bed.'

'Am I going to sleep with you?'

'Sleep with me! Good heavens, child, of course not, what an extraordinary idea! You will sleep in your own room.'

I had slept alone in a bed for the first time in my life on the boat coming to England, and it was unimaginable to me that I should sleep in a room on my own. I felt the ground begin to tilt under me.

'I do not sleep in a room by myself at home,' I said.

'I am not responsible for what you do at home. It cannot be helped, you must be patient until the other girls arrive.'

Gathering up my belongings, she took me by the hand and together we climbed the wide staircase which curved up like a tree through the middle of the house, branching off at intervals onto separate landings. On the second landing we turned left along a mile of silent corridor to the East Wing. Throwing open a door, Matron said, 'Here is your room.'

Eight iron beds stood in a line against the wall. Brown patterned cubicle curtains exactly matched the brown patterned counterpanes, and gave the room its name, The Rockery. Beside each bed was a small chest of drawers on which was a large jug and basin for washing. Beside each chest there was a small wooden chair.

Briskly she snapped open the clasps on my overnight case, and with practised hands unbuttoned me and whisked off the still unfamiliar clothes, thrust me into my new pyjamas and marched me, teeth chattering, to the lavatory, where the lavatory chain roared and rattled, and had me running headlong in fright for the door. Outside Matron was waiting to take me, even more reluctant now, back to the deserted dormitory.

'Do not forget to say your prayers,' she said. 'I shall see you in the morning. Goodnight.'

She switched off the light and left me alone for the very first time in my life: in the empty wing of that huge house in the heart of the silent countryside. Obliterated by the darkness and clamped between icy sheets, I lay immobilised; then as the sound of her footsteps retreated, fuelled by undiluted terror, I started to scream. Nobody came. Eventually I fell asleep. I was six years old and I had been in England four days.

– Chapter 6 –

Every night I was left in that empty room, and each night was more terrifying than the last. Exhausted, always cold, I passed the days in a trance, trailing through the leaves in the raw damp air, or sitting by the fire in a fog of sodden wool, my nerves strung like wire in anticipation of the moment when the light was switched out and Matron left me alone. She was impregnable. When I begged her, pounding and pulling at the steep white slopes of her uniform, to let me sleep near her, she brushed me off. When, later, she dragged my rigid body down the corridor towards my room she did not notice the skin left on the walls. If she heard my screams which followed her nightly back to the main part of the house, they did not touch her.

Dogs with dripping fangs and eyes as big as millwheels crouched on the chests of drawers beside the beds. If I so much as moved a muscle a witch might pounce from behind the cubicle curtains rustling in the wind. The window stood open for any batwinged hobgoblin to glide in on the cold currents of air. I knew from my story books that this was their territory, a land to the far north of the world, where trolls and giants prowled, ever on the lookout for unprotected children to carry off and eat. The darkness of the room was so thick it seemed to stop my breath. Each morning Matron, immaculate, returned to retrieve me like a rat from soaking sheets and dunk me, shivering and humiliated, in the bath. In the wood-panelled dining room, Miss Bowles, calm and contained in her long dark skirt and cardigan, and Miss Valentine, grittily erect in a pebbledash tweed suit, sat opposite me and enquired, 'Did you sleep well?' the one buttering a slice of thin triangular toast and the other wielding her spoon like a hammer to break open the top of her egg. Yes, I answered every day under Matron's vigilant eye. Who knew what these people might do to me if I angered them by answering otherwise; they might kill me if I wasn't careful.

However, John the groundsman, whom I was helping to sweep up the leaves before we made bonfires of them, promised me, on his honour and may God strike him dead, that Miss Bowles, Miss Valentine and Matron were not witches; nor, he said, were there trolls or any creatures of that sort in these parts. He should know because he'd lived and worked in these parts ever since he was a boy. Grandma whispered in my ear too that these people did not have the power to kill me and that I must be brave. So by the sixth day, thank goodness, there was no cause for embarrassment when Matron plucked me from my bed. As soon as I heard the other girls arriving I hid in the junior common room, where for the first time a splendid fire was blazing with flames leaping carelessly up the chimney. I took up a position behind the door, ready, if need be, to dive through the heavy chintz curtains and conceal myself in the window seat, but I kept Grandma's words in mind.

Looking through the crack in the door, I found that the hall was overflowing with all shapes and sizes of girls uniformly wrapped in nigger brown; their hands and faces livid from the cold, white, pink, and purple, they swarmed around the notice board in a continually shifting pattern against the dark wooden panelling as if someone were shaking up a great big box of sugared almonds.

I pressed my eye closer to the crack, at the same time putting up my hands to protect my ears, for the group immediately in front of me, on the other side of the door, was deafening.

'Mattie, over here, we're in Iris.'

'Jolly good, where's Primrose?'

'Haven't seen her. Hello, Angela, are you with us in Iris? I don't think I saw your name.'

'No, worse luck, Rose this term. I'm going up, see you at supper.'

A litany of flowers rang through the rafters: lupin, butter-cup, delphinium, daffodil; the dormitories were named after flowers, and so it appeared were many of their prospective occupants; Violet, Marigold, Peony, it was very confusing, particularly since they all looked identical. How would I ever be able to distinguish one from another? Among the clarion voices I heard no one call out Rockery, the name of my room, and even if I had, I had already decided that the best course of action was to stay put, preferably for ever, behind the door.

It was not to be; footsteps tapped purposefully in the now silent hall. I did not need to see her to know that Matron had come looking for me. Soon we were once again walking along the mile of corridor leading to the East Wing, but now the house was awash with light, the doors on either side were thrown wide open with girls running to and fro, and spilling from room to room as busy and as noisy as nesting starlings.

'Quiet for a moment please.' Matron raised her voice and waited dramatically in the doorway of the dormitory, very erect, balancing daintily on two of her little pink trotters, having placed the other two in the pockets of her uniform. 'I want you to welcome Remi,' she said, and produced me from behind her. 'She is a new girl and has joined us this term all the way from Africa.' She motioned me forward and I stepped into the room and into a silence in which no one breathed. My room-mates stood in a row. They examined me from top to toe; until now we could not have imagined each other. I knew their names by heart, I had studied them each day on the notice board, rolling the syllables around like marbles inside my mouth, but I had had no pictures in my head of the owners. Furthermore they resembled neither the goose girls nor princesses of my reading. We looked at one another in sheer disbelief.

'Jessica,' said Matron, 'you will take care of Remi and see that she settles in.'

'Yes, Matron,' said Jessica, who was as tall as I and with two white-blonde plaits.

I walked hesitantly towards her and sat on my bed which was next to hers in the middle of the line, relieved to be part of the group at last.

'Who is in charge of the other two new girls?' Matron enquired. There was no mistaking them either, tears were coursing down their faces more relentlessly even than the rain now falling outside. I noted this with a certain satisfaction; my crying, I thought, was done. Two veterans on either side of them stepped forward.

'We are, Matron,' they said in unison.

'Very well,' she said, and left the room.

Immediately everyone except the new girls crowded around my bed, five eager faces thrumming with curiosity and anticipation. Jessica and Anita conducted the interrogation.

'Can you speak English?' Jessica asked me kindly.

'Yes of course I can,' I replied.

'You sound quite funny,' Anita said. 'Are you really from Africa?'

'Yes, I am.'

'How did you get here?' she asked again quickly before Jessica could do so.

'Well she didn't swim, silly,' retorted Jessica, annoyed at missing her turn.

'No,' I said. 'Bigma . . . my aunt brought me.'

'Golly, when will you see your parents again?' Sarah could not resist joining in, biting a fingernail already chewed to the quick.

'I don't know,' I answered truthfully.

This was too much for Miranda, the new girl; at the mention of parents, her tears turned into loud sobs, which instantly triggered a fresh outburst in Polly, the other new girl.

Simultaneously the urgent clanging of the supper bell called us to supper, and Jessica, ignoring their sobs, seized my hand, dragged me unceremoniously out from between our beds and made a run for the door. We were almost out of the room when, louder even than the bell, another voice rang out. It stopped us in our tracks and halted the blood in our veins.

'Let go of her hand.'

Jessica dropped my hand as swiftly as if it had been a burning brand. As one, we all whirled round to see who had spoken. It was Anita. Anita was solidly built and endowed with natural gravitas, but at this moment standing in the middle of the room bathed in light, her orange plaits transformed into two rivers of flame, she had the authority of an Oracle.

'The black comes off,' she declared in a voice of doom. 'If you touch her the black will rub off on you and very soon you will be black all over too.'

Transfixed, we stared in alarm, first at me, even I looked down at me, and then at Jessica's hand, half expecting it to turn black before our very eyes.

'No it doesn't,' I said. 'It doesn't come off.'

'Yes it does,' said Anita. 'My Aunt Jane said so. She told my brother that if he didn't behave himself she would send him to Africa and the black would rub off all the people there onto him.'

'That's not true, it doesn't come off. Look,' I said, rubbing the back of my hand frantically with the other one which I then turned over palm upwards for them to see. Horror of horrors, my palm of course was pink, and the lines on it very distinct and dark. The black had quite clearly rubbed off.

'You see,' said Anita, and her manner proclaimed: Ladies of the jury, I rest my case. Rapidly a space cleared around me, and now as we hurried off to supper, Jessica merely turned and said over her shoulder, 'Come on, follow me.'

This evening the character of the dining room was altered too; it was friendlier, cut down to size, filled now as it was meant to be with three hundred girls crammed closely together at the long wooden tables. It seemed to me that the ceiling had come down a foot or two, the lights shone brighter and the portraits on the wall looked less forbidding. The din of renewed acquaintance would have put the Jankara market mammies to shame.

I was the subject of intense interest when I arrived, heads craned and all eyes followed me as I lined up with the others to be served. I kept my eyes firmly on the centre of Jessica's straight back, and followed her as closely as a baby chick its mother, looking neither to left nor to right, until we were safely sitting down. Even then I kept my eyes glued to my plate and tried to keep as motionless as possible in case I accidentally knocked against one of my neighbours, dreading that at any moment Anita might jump up before all these people and tell them that the black came off. And so, rendered deaf and dumb, I let the girls from my dormitory speak for me.

'What's your name?'

I didn't answer.

'She's called Remi,' said Jessica.

'And she comes from darkest Africa,' said Anita, flicking first one plait and then the other over her shoulder.

'Ooooh,' came collectively from those staring goggle-eyed at me across the table.

Darkest Africa, this was new to me. They must imagine, I thought, that Africa was like England, shrouded, as it had been since the day I arrived, in almost perpetual darkness. Really Anita knew nothing about Africa.

'It may not be Darkest Africa,' Jessica said, 'we don't know where from exactly.'

'Her English sounds rather peculiar,' piped Minnie in her little voice.

'And she's got no parents,' Sarah said, 'she came here all by herself.'

As I would not be drawn and continued as it were to play dead, I soon ceased to be of interest, and general conversation was resumed. I sat with the other two new girls in contemplative silence. The only signs of life from them were sniffs and stifled sobs, and it was not difficult to guess what occupied their thoughts. I on the other hand was now conditioned to be less ambitious. Instead of wishing I could be back at home, I only wanted to be back safely behind the door of the junior sitting room.

Grandma would have been disappointed – she would have expected me to speak up for myself – and Yowande would have been scornful. It was easy for them, they were safe at home.

Anita did not like me and she made sure the rumour that my colour came off spread through the whole of the junior school. No one would come near me at first and when they did, they took elaborate care not to brush against me. She was jealous, I could tell, of her friendship with Jessica, who on account of her beauty was the undisputed queen. Jessica was a watersprite whose hair gleamed silver and whose white skin shone green in the hollows of her elbows and knees where the ribbons of her veins were threaded through. From the very first night, and despite Anita's awful warning, she had given every indication in sidelong looks and glances, and an interest in everything I had to say, that she was as fascinated by me as I was by her. I didn't blame Anita, in fact I could not help admiring her for the blackness trick, it was smart; had the situation been reversed and we had been in Lagos, I would have done the same and so would Yowande. I knew too from Yowande's experience when she first arrived in Grandpa's house, that you could not expect to be accepted straight away, you had to prove yourself first. The other new girls cried every time they were teased and, would you believe, told tales. They would have known never to do that if they had lived in the house on Bamgbose Street.

I was not as unhappy as I might have been. Mama wrote to me and Grandma wrote too; they loved me and missed me, they said, and they were sure I had made new friends. I told them about Jessica, Anita and the other two girls who made up the fearsome four. Sarah I regarded with awe: she ate absolutely everything, including my two-day-old sago pudding which, sneaking into the dining room, she wolfed for me as I sat alone in front of it in the evening. In summer, I wrote, she had so many freckles she resembled a lawn full of daisies. Minnie was skinny and supple as a piece of string; she reminded me, I told Yowande, of my youngest nanny, Alaba. I described them because I was certain you see that it was only a matter of time . . .

I did not tell them in my letters home, though, of how famous I had become in the junior school, or why. To begin with, in my stories of 'life in Africa', I naturally described the house in Lagos, but I soon discovered that this was not the way to keep the interest of my schoolfriends. What they required, and for which they developed an apparently insatiable appetite, was life in the African wild. My experience of such being nil, I was forced to invent, and the well would very soon have dried had I not been able to replenish it from an unexpected source which I had found in Croydon.

Uncle Theo and Aunty Betty, who were my Guardians and with whom I stayed in the holidays, lived in Stanley Terrace in Thornton Heath. Their son Gerald took after his mother's side, and her family's characteristic, gigantism, made him by natural selection the leader of the Stanley Terrace gang. He insisted right away that I join; only as an honorary member, though, because I didn't live there all the time. I'd be honoured, I said.

'Come on then, come and meet them,' he said, and, having finished his tea, he leapt up, making the empty plates jump too on Aunty Betty's spotless white tablecloth.

He yanked me bodily from my seat and, keeping a firm grip on my neck, dragged me unceremoniously out of the house and through the gate which led into the narrow alleyway separating our gardens, the territory of the Stanley Terrace gang, from those of our deadly enemies the Clarence Street gang. The alley as well as being our meeting place was also Lover's Lane, and the lovers, though protected by high fences and hedges from prying eyes in the gardens, were forced to conduct their tenderest moments beneath our cynical gaze.

'She's just a baby,' Doreen said, 'she talks funny – it don't even sound like English to me – and – '

But before she could finish, Roger, who had been staring at me, horrified, finished for her. 'She's a darkie! I don't think we should have one of them in with us.'

'We'll never hear the end of it from the Clarence Street mob,' Wilf said. 'They'll laugh theirselves silly.'

Paula put on a knowing expression but said nothing, she lived next door to Gerald and would be close to his wrath should things not go his way, so she was in a delicate position.

Gerald pointed out that on the contrary, far from making them a laughing stock, my being a member of the gang would lend a unique authenticity to the Tarzan games which were played by both gangs after Saturday morning pictures.

'Just think,' he said, 'we would have the real thing, a genuine African savage.'

Furthermore, Gerald said, when the occasion demanded it, I could double up as a Red Indian, savages being the same the world over, he reckoned.

'You'd like that, wouldn't you?' he said, looking down at me kindly.

I didn't want Doreen to know that I had never heard of Tarzan or Red Indians so I said, 'Of course, I'd like that very much.' Thus it was settled.

Saturday morning pictures were a revelation to me and although I was still keen to play my part, I was confused by certain aspects of the film we had just seen, much to the irritation of Doreen who wanted to get on with the game. We were assembled in the alley prior to starting.

'Why did Tarzan choose to live with the animals in the jungle rather than with the people?' I asked.

'That's because they're darkies,' Doreen said.

Not wanting to let on that I was ignorant of the significance of this fact, I said, 'I know that, but animals can't talk. Tarzan must be pretty stupid to stay with them all the time.'

'What you have to understand, dumbo,' Gerald said, affectionately ruffling my hair, 'is that Tarzan was brought up by animals, his foster mother was a chimp.'

'He was brought up by a monkey?' I asked in disbelief.

'Yes, that's why he gets on better with animals. He understands them and they understand him. He doesn't really trust people.'

'So what will happen when he wants to marry?'

'He marries Jane,' Paula said patiently.

'When they are married, will Tarzan and Jane go and live in the village like everyone else?' I persisted.

'I told you before, they don't want to go and live with the darkies.'

This time I looked to Gerald. 'Why don't they?'

'Don't worry about it,' he said, 'it's just that English people are daft about animals, everyone knows that. You just do what I tell you and everything will work out. OK?'

'OK,' I said.

The Tarzan films proved invaluable at school (no one else at Chilcott Manor attended Saturday morning pictures). By and by my father metamorphosed into a tribal chieftain whose frequent duty it was to leave his house in Lagos in order to make ceremonial visits to his ancestral village deep in the heart of the jungle, and when I was in Africa I used to accompany him, naturally, with the rest of his household. Papa would have been amazed to hear, as I sat by the fire toasting crumpets, how frequently he led his villagers out on a leopard hunt with only his spear to protect him. Mama, Grandma and Patience would have been equally astounded to hear that only the day before they had been sitting in the open around a snake stew supper. Who could tell what they might be doing tomorrow?

'Gerald,' I said, shortly before I left Croydon for the start of the autumn term and the beginning of the new school year, 'you know Doreen didn't want me in the Stanley Terrace gang because I'm a darkie?' I was wiser now.

'Yeah.' Gerald was delicately putting a propeller onto one of his balsa wood aeroplanes, it was finicky work.

'Well they don't want me to join in at school either for the same reason. They say the black rubs off. What do you think I can do about it?'

'Knock their blocks off,' Gerald said.

Yowande would have approved of Gerald, but it was, unfortunately, not proving as simple for me at school as it had been with the Stanley Terrace gang in Croydon. I was being ostracised, not in lessons or at meal times where the mistresses could see but in the interstices of the day when we were left to ourselves, where, as I had been quick to realise, the real business of school was conducted: in the private games we played.

Mademoiselle, the French assistant, discovered me in tears. It seemed I had not, as I had written in my letters, done with crying after all. I had concealed myself where I hoped I would not be heard, on the blue bench. Normally we sat there only when we were sent out of class for misbehaviour. The bench was set against the wall in the long curve beneath the staircase, and twenty minutes in the bone-chilling gloominess of the hall, affording us, as Miss Valentine said, a salutary glimpse of purgatory, was more than enough to make us repent of our sins and promise anything to be allowed back into the warmth. For once I was indifferent to the cold, and I lay on my back on the bench, slowly turning to stone like an effigy on a tomb, while tears trickled down the sides of my face and onto the blue tapestry cushion. I had broken finally.

'Who is there? Remi, what are you doing there?' Mademoiselle came and sat down beside me. When I continued to cry she pulled me up against her and said, 'What is the matter, come, you can tell me, what is it?'

'The black doesn't come off,' I said, sobbing.

'What did you say?'

'Anita's aunt says that the black comes off, and it doesn't, does it?'

'I do not understand what you are speaking about, let us take this slowly, what black?'

'The black on me.'

'*Mon dieu*, you mean the colour of your skin?'

'They think it will rub off on them and so . . . and so no one will play with me.'

'First of all you can be sure of one thing, the black absolutely does not come off, you do not believe that, do you?'

'No,' I said, wiping my eyes.

'In that case stop crying now and dry your eyes. Everything we will arrange tomorrow in the French lesson.'

'*Bonjour, Mesdemoiselles*,' she greeted us crisply on entering the classroom carrying her books on her arm.

'*Bonjour, Mademoiselle*,' we chanted back.

'*Asseyez-vous, s'il vous plaît.*'

We sat down, having exhausted our entire stock of newly acquired French vocabulary. Mademoiselle took her place at the table on the raised platform at the top of the room and faced us for the first lesson after lunch.

'Before I begin our lesson today, I wish you all to listen to me very carefully,' she began. 'There has been an unfortunate mistake relating to one of the pupils in this form, Remi, who has joined us as you know from Africa. You will no doubt be taught in your geography lesson what I will tell you, but I think it is very important that you should know this now.'

Anita coughed loudly and ostentatiously and tossed her head. I resolutely examined the hieroglyphics carved by previous generations on the lid of my desk, and I could have sworn there were red ants crawling up the back of my neck.

Mademoiselle proceeded to explain to us clearly and succinctly why our skins were different colours and why those colours did not come off.

'But,' said Anita, 'did my aunt tell a lie?'

'Your aunt did not mean what she said,' said Mademoiselle, 'she only wanted to frighten you. It was not a sensible thing to do.'

With that she stepped down from the platform, hugged me and then, laughing, ruffled my hair. The pale winter sun trickled in through the high leaded windows and struck answering glints from Mademoiselle's magnificent golden tooth.

From that moment on I adored Mademoiselle, and I never wavered in my adoration even when the entire form developed a crush on Miss Flood, the new games mistress, with whom Mademoiselle could not hope to compete. Miss Flood's profile, so our history teacher said, was classic Greek; in spite of being a Protestant from Bergerac, Mademoiselle had a classic Mediterranean moustache and bandy legs.

I turned the tables on Anita as we were getting ready for bed. When she reached for her pyjama case I suddenly cried out, 'Oh be careful, the green comes off!' mimicking her voice and every move until I had reduced the dormitory to hysterics with even Jessica stuffing her pillow in her mouth to prevent the giggles out of loyalty to her best friend. Poor Anita was reduced to sitting immobile in the middle of her bed, not daring to move a muscle or touch a thing, just as I had been on that first evening in the dining room. I wish Yowande could have been there, she would have been proud of me.

The spell had been broken and, combined with my lethal ability on the games field (there wasn't a ball I could not run down, hit or catch), there was no limit to my success, everyone wanted to be my friend. Only the fearsome four, held back by Anita, failed to succumb, but I was confident she would not be able to hold them for long. Inexorably, day by day, they too were being drawn towards me: 'Let's pretend,' I said, 'we are in a boat on the Niger river . . .' or 'Just suppose this was the jungle . . .' No one else could match the glamour and excitement of my games, I was confident that the four would soon be five. The catalyst was my quarrel with Estelle Matthews, ending in a fight in the corridor outside the middle school common room, and occurred even sooner than I had anticipated. Estelle had also come from Africa, but she was not, she said, from Darkest Africa. We still had not established exactly where that was, but we were now pretty certain that I was not from there; I had proved to the satisfaction of my classmates that my home was blindingly bright and sunny, that wasn't in dispute. What was disputed were my stories of life in Lagos. Estelle lived in South Africa, a place which I personally had never heard of, and only Anita, through her famous Aunt Jane, who had lived there also, knew of its existence. Estelle claimed that in her part of Africa, Africans were only employed as servants and she did not believe that my grandfather could possibly have had Europeans working for him. Each of us accused the other vehemently of lying, which led in a trice to my hauling on her plaits as hard as I could and her burying her hands in my cropped mop and attempting to roll it back like turf in order to settle the matter properly.

'What is the meaning of this?' Miss Bowles's sibilant whisper effortlessly penetrated the din made by our cheering supporters, who fell silent instantly, 'What has been going on here?' Nobody answered. 'Very well. You, Remi, and you, Estelle, shall go and sit on the blue bench until it is time for supper. I will not countenance this kind of uncivilised behaviour in my school, is that understood?'

'Yes, Miss Bowles.'

We sat in chilled silence until rescued by the supper bell when, cramped and stiff but still unyielding, we joined the others in the dining room where the controversy still raged and continued to do so while we waited for lights out.

It was then that Jessica said, 'I believe Remi, she's the one who really comes from Africa, she should know, don't you agree, Anita?'

Anita was crosslegged on her bed, minutely inspecting the pattern of orange teddy bears on her blue pyjamas. From behind the curtain of her orange hair she said, 'Yes, I suppose so.'

'So do I,' said Minnie.

'Me too.' Sarah's voice was muffled, she was eating a piece of bread she had smuggled from supper, hidden in the handkerchief pocket of her bloomers.

You see, Grandma whispered in my ear, it was only a matter of time.

My apotheosis was completed on Sports Day at the end of the summer term but the event was somewhat overshadowed by the attendance of Aunty Betty. Loitering around waiting for her, I was accosted by Rosie Barnes's parents; she was in the fourth form.

'Hallo,' her mother said to me, 'you must be the little girl from Africa.'

'Uh huh.' I was non-committal.

'And where are your parents, my dear?'

You didn't have to be a genius to see they weren't there. 'They are at home.'

'In Africa, I dare say. My, that is a long way away. How often do you see them?'

'Never.' I scowled, hoping to close the matter. I hated these conversations.

'Good gracious! Why is that, do you suppose?'

I looked up at the sky, forgive me God. 'They are dead,' I said. 'Excuse me, I see my aunt arriving.'

I was delighted to see Aunty Betty and I took her immediately across to Miss Bowles who was talking with a group of parents and proudly introduced her. Miss Bowles said how kind it was of Aunty Betty to attend our sports day and she hoped this was the first of many visits she would be paying us at school.

'Pleased to meet you,' Aunty Betty said. 'Very kind of you, I'm sure.'

A silence had fallen on our arrival and now everyone was staring, fascinated, at Aunty Betty. She did look different from the other parents. In spite of the day being rather warm she was dressed, as was usual for her, in a dark brown coat, a cloche hat pulled well down, thick lisle stockings and solid brown shoes, beautifully polished by Uncle Theo, I suspected, which made allowances for her bunions. I took her away quickly to watch the start of the races.

'Where did you say you lived?' Anita's mother asked, pressing her large straw hat down on her head in case it blew off in the breeze. She had pursued us across the grass and her flowered dress rustled busily as she took her place beside us on the sidelines; so interested was she in Aunty Betty, she almost missed Anita coming sixteenth in the sack race.

'I didn't,' Aunty Betty said.

'Well where *do* you live?' She was not to be put off.

'Thornton 'eath,' Aunty Betty conceded. 'You 'ave to change at Clapham Junction.'

'Really?' Anita's mother said.

I felt quite sorry for Aunty Betty. All afternoon she attracted even more attention than me, which was not easy because I won every event in my age group and the one above for my house, Druid. Walking with her in between the races, it was as if a giraffe had magically materialised at my side. I do believe that Grandma in full Yoruba costume would have excited less curiosity.

Aunty Betty didn't seem to mind too much though, and at the end of all the ceremonies when, clutching my handful of ribbons, I was chaired by my friends, one of whom was Anita, she said she couldn't have been prouder if it was one of her own. Grandma would have been proud of me too, and Mama and Patience. Yowande might have been a little jealous, I thought.

It seemed as if the little pot of African clay, which had been sent bobbing thousands of miles across the ocean, had survived against all the odds intact; the brown glaze was as shiny as before, only the hairline crack running from top to bottom on the inside betrayed that it was not the same as it was and would never be again.

– Chapter 7 –

Three years had passed since Aunty Betty's first sports day at Chilcott Manor, four years altogether since I'd been in England and, as Aunty Betty said, my own mother would not have recognised me now. Doreen of the Stanley Terrace gang disagreed; as far as she was concerned nothing was changed, I was years younger than the rest of them, I still talked funny – only now it was all posh and ladidah, on account of that fancy school I went to – and I was still a darkie whatever anyone said. Gerald had no business foisting me on them every holiday like he did. She did not, of course, say this to Gerald's face. Jessica and my friends at school said that I was now so English it was impossible to imagine that I had actually been born in Africa. This was true, but it was also true that I now understood what a darkie was and a native and a savage, which had led, to use Miss Valentine's expression, to a lamentable change in my behaviour. There had for example been the little incident with Rosie Barnes's mother. Miss Valentine was unable to conceive how any child could be so wicked as to wish her parents dead. I hadn't wished my parents dead, I said, I had merely wanted to avoid yet another set of prying questions, which had earned me half an hour on the blue bench. The fight with Estelle Matthews had been at my instigation, Miss Bowles said. She had been rude about Africans, I replied. That was no reason, Miss Bowles said, to engage in fisticuffs. Miss Miles was not amused, she said, by my cheeky contradictions in her lessons, however much they entertained the rest of the class. My suggestion that Mungo Park might have fared better in his voyage down the Niger if he'd asked the way from the people already there was but one example, she told Miss Flood, the games mistress, who regretted the time spent on the blue bench away from the playing field.

Mama wrote to say that I had two new sisters, Yejide and Yinka, making us five children now in all, which was nice of course, but I was more concerned that I would never see Boswell the Great Dane again. I was not surprised though, remembering Baba Cook's attitude, to hear that he had died. Sarah, when I told her this, was more inclined to side with Baba Cook. There was a lot of meat on a Great Dane, she said. Minnie found Sarah's lust for food disgusting, but Anita said it wasn't her fault, she was deprived because of being a war baby. My father, who wrote to me only at the beginning and end of every term, was concerned at the recent and extraordinary deterioration in my behaviour, as attested in my school reports. He could not imagine the cause, he said, but the decline must stop forthwith. He had no quarrel with my academic results, high marks were to be expected in one from our family. Grandma wrote that Nimota had married Kemi, so Mama Ibeji's spell bought all that time ago from Jankara market must have been successful after all. Anita was not surprised, she had heard of similar happenings in England, she said.

'Yes,' I said, 'like the spell you put on me on my first day at school.'

'You could take it,' Anita said.

'Stop that, you two,' Jessica intervened. 'We were all very young then, none of us would believe such nonsense now.'

Grandma also wrote that Alaba, my youngest nanny, had returned to her village to be married, and that Yowande was receiving rather better school reports than mine, by all accounts, at the CMS School in Lagos.

In my letters I asked my mother why, in all this time, I had not returned home. She replied that Papa believed an English education to be the best thing for me and best acquired in England, and so, as it was necessary for me to be in England to attend school, I might as well take advantage of the holidays too to absorb all I could. He would have thought it very selfish to bring me to Nigeria, she said, simply because they all missed me, when I was in a good position to better myself in England. That was all very well, but my friends were convinced I must have done something very wrong for my family to have abandoned me in this fashion. I was beginning to think so too and what I most desired in this last week of term, as the four of us idled on the grass beneath the lime trees, was a letter from my father declaring that this summer, English education notwithstanding, I would be going home for the holidays. The weather was very close and from time to time drops of sticky juice fell from the leaves onto our heads and uncovered legs as we lay with our summer shorts pulled up well above our knees. Thoughts of the holidays were uppermost in all our minds.

'What are you doing this summer, Remi?' Anita asked.

I appeared not to have heard her.

'Surely you will be going home this year, won't you?' Sarah said. She was carefully dismembering a white clover flower, and sucking the sweetness at the root of each tiny petal.

'I'm not sure what I'll be doing this summer.' I examined a blade of grass, feigning disinterest.

'Haven't you heard from your father? It's getting rather late, isn't it?' Anita persisted.

I wanted very much to slap her.

'There's plenty of time.' Jessica sat up slowly as if surfacing from a pool. 'A whole week yet.' Then, turning to me, she said, 'Race you to the pavilion,' and dashed away across the playing field. I chased gratefully after her.

My father wrote that I would not be going to Lagos for the summer holidays, I would be staying in Croydon as usual with Uncle Theo and Aunty Betty. He never gave me a reason and I did not expect one from him. I examined the letter again and again in the hope that in the interval, somehow, the words would have arranged themselves to read that I would be going home after all; that there on the quayside would be Mama, Grandma and Patience waving and welcoming me back. No miracle occurred. I folded the letter for the last time and hurried along to the Long Gallery where the Upper Fifth were putting on an end of term performance of *Pride and Prejudice*. Barbara McKenzie, my idol, was playing Mr Darcy and Lizzie Browne, whom Jessica admired, was appearing as Elizabeth Bennet.

'My mother is not very well, so I won't be going to Lagos this summer,' I told Anita as we took our seats.

'Ah,' she said sceptically, 'how sad.'

'I'm sure your mother will be better by next year,' Jessica said, 'and then you will be able to go home.'

'Yes, I expect so,' I replied as the lights went down.

It was a superb production, everybody said so. Mr Darcy was particularly dashing, and I would forever picture him with bright red hair, jet black brows and a magnificent thirty-eight-inch bust.

Chilcott Manor and elocution lessons had taught me to be ashamed of Aunty Betty and Croydon, and ever since her first visit to school I had been deliberately vague when questioned about my holidays. It would have been very unfair on Gerald, I felt, to have people making fun of his mother. I was in love with Gerald. This did not prevent the words of my elocution mistress impressing themselves upon my mind.

'Where on earth . . . do you spend your holidays, my dear?' she asked me early on.

'Thornton 'eath, Croydon,' I replied.

'My dear Remi,' she said, tossing back her head and clasping her arms dramatically across her breast so that her ivory bracelets, from wrist to elbow, clashed like cymbals and her hair flew out in a purple cloud, 'if you wish to succeed in England, you must never mention that place; and certainly never breathe a word of it to me again, do you hear?'

Having successfully razed to the ground my, as she called them, 'towering Nigerian vowels', Miss Clifford-Broughton was driven distraught at the start of each term by the South London ones, which popped up like mole hills on the immaculate lawns of my new diction.

So as the school train pulled into Victoria Station, I stuck my head out of the window with the others, more as a matter of form than out of conviction or anticipation. Immediately I spied Aunty Betty looming up in the distance, massive and unmoving in dark grey, as if she were actually set into the ground, like a commemorative group statue cast in bronze.

The rest of the parents streamed loudly past Aunty Betty onto the platform, laughing and shouting to each other in clear confident voices as they rushed to reclaim their offspring running noisily towards them down the length of the train. I did not rush: like Aunty Betty I stood quite still, both of us dark silent rocks against which the stream swirled and eddied and finally receded in a flurry of goodbyes.

When the moment could be delayed no longer, I moved slowly up the platform clutching my overnight case, weaving in and out among the stragglers, while Aunty Betty charted my progress unblinking. At last I stood beside her and she inclined her head towards me.

'Aren't you going to give me a kiss, Remi?' she said.

I looked round uneasily. Not everyone had gone, indeed Rosie Barnes's parents were staring at us as usual as if transfixed.

'Surely you're going to give me a kiss,' Aunty Betty repeated more loudly, and, fearful of attracting any more attention, I hastily planted a kiss on her cheek, which she presented by leaning straight forward from the hips. She was unable to bend at the waist on account of her corsets.

'That's better,' she said, creaking upright and then back down again in order to pick up my case which lay between us on the ground. I nodded to Rosie, and, ignoring her parents, followed Aunty Betty at a distance as she made her way like a giant turtle to where we were to catch the train to Croydon, changing at Clapham Junction. At the beginning of every holiday, it was much as it had been on the very first occasion when she had opened the door on Bigmama and me in my oversize rubber raincoat. We stole surreptitious glances at each other as the train rattled its way through the fine summer afternoon.

'How was school this term?' Aunty Betty asked after a long silence.

'Fine,' I said.

'You've got the hang of it now I suppose?'

'Yes.'

'I expect you're glad to be coming home though.'

Politeness demanded I say yes. 'Yes,' I said.

I was glad not to be left at school at any rate, though bitterly disappointed not to be going home to Lagos.

'I've made you your favourite lunch,' she said.

My heart sank. Aunty Betty had once asked me what I liked best to eat, and I had replied, rice.

'That's all right then,' she had said, 'you won't find anyone makes a better rice pudding than me, will she, Theo?'

'You're not wrong there,' Uncle Theo agreed.

'What is rice pudding?' I had demanded.

'It's rice baked in the oven with milk and sugar.'

'Ugh!' I said. 'I like rice with soup.'

'Soup?' said Aunty Betty.

Uncle Theo had scratched his head and then, inspired, had said, 'Maybe she means gravy, like a curry, like they eat in India. Can you describe it?' he asked, turning to me.

'Oh yes,' I said, 'it's just soup.'

Aunty Betty persevered and she had to her satisfaction mastered my 'favourite' food, boiled rice pudding covered in brown gravy. The only problem was that I now liked sausage and chips best. I looked across at her and dutifully asked, 'What have you cooked for lunch, Aunty?'

'Rice and soup,' she replied, smiling.

'Scrumptious,' I said.

We both turned back to watching the afternoon roll by.

Stanley Terrace was rather more appealing in the summer; although there were no trees, the all-over grey was splashed with colour from the roses, hollyhocks and lupins bursting out of the tiny front garden.

'That's a relief,' Aunty Betty said as she shut the door, and we were standing in the dark coolness of the hall. 'You go on up, Remi. I've put a frock for you to wear on your bed, and when you've finished you can come and help me get these corsets off. It's that hot today.'

I left her fanning herself with her grey straw and raced up the stairs to the bedroom which I shared with her daughter, Maureen, and which overlooked the garden at the back. Straight away I leant out of the window to take in Uncle Theo's roses which Aunty Betty maintained were the best in England. She frequently remarked that Uncle Theo would surely go to heaven for his roses if for nothing else. It was a pretty room, all blue, and Maureen's bed and mine under the window were both covered with blue candlewick counterpanes. There was a blue flower pattern rug floating on the shiny glass sea of the lino.

Aunty Betty polished all the lino in the house into a state of dangerous slipperiness, but we were saved from broken limbs by the rubber grip carpet slippers she made us wear inside the house. They kept us firmly suctioned to the floor. We were also obliged, the minute we arrived in the house, to take all our clothes off. Best clothes, Aunty Betty said, were for going out in, and as long as we were clean it didn't matter what we wore about the house.

I was delighted to throw off my blazer and panama hat, and exchange my school gingham for the gingham laid out on the bed. In the holidays I wore the handed down school dresses of Paula next door which, Aunty Betty said, saved my poor father money. I didn't mind, a change was as good as a rest, but I could imagine what Aunt Rose would have said had she seen me as I contemplated my reflection in the triple glass of Maureen's dressing table.

I resisted the temptation to dab on a little 'Evening in Paris' because I didn't want to use it all up myself having given it as a present to Maureen on her birthday. I bought it from Woolworths and she said when I gave it to her that it was her favourite scent. I liked it too, mainly because of the bottle which was midnight blue with a picture of the Eiffel tower on the label, picked out in white. Then I stepped out across the landing to help Aunty Betty out of her corsets.

Aunty Betty had two distinct silhouettes and both were

equally awe-inspiring. Outside, she was never seen without her corsets, which were boned and spiked like a palisade. Her flesh flowed out over the top of them in a big roll around her body. This forced her arms to stick straight out from her sides and made her look exactly the same in front as behind. When she had on one of her favourite cloche hats, you could only tell if she were coming or going by observing in which direction her feet were pointing.

Inside, she always took her corsets off. 'Quickly, undo the laces for me,' she said, turning her back in readiness, looking I thought like a genie stuck in a barrel, and when I pulled the laces and set her free, I felt a rush of power as if I were a magician.

I often wondered, having discussed the practicalities of procreation in relation to our parents with my schoolfriends, how Uncle Theo had actually begot Maureen and Gerald with Aunty Betty, because it seemed to me that if she were dressed, and he were suddenly seized with passion, as Anita reliably informed us he might be, it would have been like making advances to the front elevation of a cathedral, or if she were undressed, Uncle Theo might have had better luck attempting an assault on the North Face of the Eiger.

Aged nine, however, I merely thought Aunty Betty, un-trammelled, was as big as Australia. I also thought when we sat down to lunch, and I saw the delicious looking apple pie which was to follow my 'favourite' rice, that she was not a bad old thing really.

I had no hope of seeing any of my Croydon friends, in particular Gerald, until teatime because they were all still at school. Their term wouldn't end for a week. So when lunch was finished, I sat on the swing and swooned among the roses while the sun made butterfly patterns through my closed eyelids. Until I was awakened shockingly by two sticky hands laid heavily over my eyes accompanied by the piercing sing-song of Paula from next door demanding, 'Guess who, guess who?'

'Doreen, take your hands away,' I said to annoy her.

'It's not Doreen, guess again,' she said.

'I can't. Who is it?'

'It's me – Paula,' she said, taking her hands away. 'Couldn't you tell?'

'Yes, of course I could,' I said, laughing. 'I was only teasing.'

'When did you get back then?'

'This morning.'

'We don't finish until next week, you're the lucky one aren't you, Miss.'

She pushed the swing violently so that I fell off.

I lunged for her and within seconds we were scrabbling on the grass.

'Paula, Paula, come in this minute, you'll get your dress filthy and you've got to wear it again tomorrow,' screamed her mother, who could see us from her kitchen window. Reluctantly, Paula let go of my arm and ran to the bottom of the garden where there was a tiny gap in the roses and she could scramble over the fence without being ripped to shreds on the thorns.

'See you after tea in the alley,' she said as she bounded away.

I hurried inside too, smoothing down my dress and rubbing at the grass stains. If Paula was home then Gerald might be too. In fact he was most probably indoors right now gobbling down his tea in his usual fashion without even bothering to come outside and say hallo.

'Oh there you are,' Aunty Betty said as I pushed open the door of the kitchen. 'I was just going to call you in for your tea. Gerald's eating his already.' As if I didn't know.

'Thank you, Aunty,' I said sweetly, 'can I carry anything into the dining room for you?'

'Yes,' said Aunty, looking a little surprised, 'you can take those scones in, over there on the side.'

'Hallo, Gerald.' I gave him my best smile over the scones, sidled in and sat down opposite him at the table.

'Oh hallo,' said Gerald looking up, while his spoon which he held like a starting handle in his huge hand continued its seamless circular journey carrying rhubarb and custard from his plate to his face without a pause.

106

'You back? More's the pity,' he said grinning.

'Would you like a scone? I could butter one for you,' I said.

'Would you like a scone?' he replied, mimicking me. 'Blimey, what do they do to you at that school? "I could butter you one." You get worse and worse every time you come home.' And he roared with laughter.

'Now now, Gerald,' Aunty Betty said, coming in with a fresh pot of tea, 'you leave her alone, they're teaching her to talk lovely, I only wish my Maureen spoke half as good. It wouldn't do you no harm either to have some elocution lessons.'

'Downright cissy if you ask me,' said Gerald, nabbing the proffered scone. Aunty Betty had baked a special tea for my homecoming, and both of us watched fondly as it disappeared down Gerald.

'What are you staring at me like that for?' Gerald demanded.

'No reason, and I wasn't staring.'

'Yes, you were and pretty miserable you looked too.'

'Leave her alone, Gerald, I expect she hoped she might be going home to Africa this time, didn't you?' Aunty Betty turned to me.

'Not especially.' I shook my head and traced a pattern on the tablecloth.

'Can I get you any more tea?'

I shook my head again.

'Last orders, please, before I clear away.' Aunty Betty began to gather the plates.

'Cheer up, girl. We're going to have a good time this summer, Mum's outdone herself. Go on, tell 'er.' Gerald nudged his mother's elbow and winked at me.

'I was saving it up as a surprise, Gerald, until nearer the time. You've let the cat out now. Well, Remi, I've booked us in for a fortnight by the sea this year not just for the week, and . . . instead of the boarding house in Brighton, I've taken a caravan at Mudeford-on-Sea. We're all going: Aunty Madge and Uncle Reg, and Mavis and Alec from Uncle Theo's lot; my sister Peggy, her husband Bert and their daughter Dorcas who

I know you like.' (I did not like Dorcas at all, she always complained that I tagged on to her and Gerald.)

'What about Maureen?' I asked.

'She's staying here by herself, she's twenty-one and can do as she pleases.' Aunty Betty was clearly disappointed in Maureen.

'Let's go and spread the good news.' Gerald jumped up from the table, grabbing me by the neck as usual. 'Roger will be hopping mad when he hears we're taking a caravan for a fortnight and so will his mum, that'll teach 'em to have a name instead of a number on their house.' He was popping with glee.

My joy, as I was dragged down the garden slung in a poacher's grip like a rabbit, was not unalloyed: I found the seaside in England miserably cold and there was little doubt in my mind that people would gawp at me in Mudeford much as they did in Brighton where I had drawn crowds in previous years.

According to the brochure, Mudeford, although new, was a lively little resort recently reclaimed from the sea between Christchurch and Bournemouth. The caravan site was new too and the planks which had been put down as walkways connecting the caravans to the rest of Mudeford were currently being reclaimed by the mud which squelched over the tops of our shoes when we stepped onto them. We were joined the morning after we arrived by the rest of Gerald's aunts and uncles, having travelled down ourselves with Aunty Betty's sister Peggy and Uncle Bert. Their daughter Dorcas complained bitterly all the way down on the train that she wished she could have stayed at home like Maureen. She was not the only one, Gerald said under his breath. Aunty Peggy said she had a long way to go before she was twenty-one, Miss, and could have a key to the door, and Aunty Betty said it would have been a pity if Dorcas had stayed away, because she knew how much I had been looking forward to her company. Yes, I said. I was a liar, Gerald said under his breath again. It was all very well for him but I had Aunty Peggy to contend with.

Sitting silently in my corner, I concentrated on the brochure, which had nice pictures not exactly reminiscent of Mudeford, and refused to be goaded by the jibes and taunts tossed down less frequently now by my watchers on the other side of the windbreak.

'Hey, you lot, bugger off before I crack your heads open,' Gerald, back momentarily foraging for food, shouted at the children in his characteristically forceful way, straddling the entrance like a Goliath.

'Now, now, Gerald,' said Aunty Betty, handing him a sandwich and lowering herself again into a nervous-looking deck chair, 'there's no need for bad language.'

Encouraged, the children swarmed like flies. But Gerald had not come to the seaside to act as a fly swat. Before long he lost interest in our audience, and, brushing them aside contemptuously, he made his way swiftly back to the sea, leaving me to sit it out as best I could, and who could blame him?

'There's rings in his ears,' said one of my tormentors, craning right inside to look at me.

'Oh yeah, so there is,' said another.

'Do you suppose he's got a tail?' asked a third.

'Dunno, can't see from here,' said the first one again, this time staring straight into my eyes.

I decided to ignore the comments just this once. I was tired temporarily of defending the honour of Africa. Reflecting glumly that in Mudeford I looked set to break all my previous records, I dug myself deeper into my corner and, observing Gerald's family, I was reminded of mine.

The pink-painted house in Bamgbose Street would be shimmering now in the afternoon heat, and inside it would be warm and dark. Grandma would be stationed in her rocking chair in the corner of the sitting room by her bedroom door, her fine silk dress smoothed over her lap, and her hair plaited in a white corolla around her head. Aunt Rose would be sitting beside her, thin and insubstantial as a shadow; both of them ready for what the day would bring. Through the windows of the long dining room they would be able to hear the foster children playing under the mango trees and smell the corn being roasted in the outside kitchen. Grandma's lap where I used to sit would be empty.

Gerald's aunts and uncles sat in a semicircle facing the sea, the uncles on one side and the aunts on the other. Uncle Theo lay sprawled between Uncle Bert and Uncle Alec. All three of them and Uncle Reg on the far side were fast asleep, their stomachs rising and falling in unison between their braces, and their curled pink feet exposed to the elements were like shelled crabs resting on the sand. They had abandoned their jackets and rolled up their sleeves. In place of his usual cap Uncle Theo had knotted a large white handkerchief and put it over his head in case the sun should come out.

The aunts on the other hand were wide awake and talking, the gossip flowing backwards and forwards keeping pace with their knitting. As I watched I fervently hoped that Aunty Betty was not making another bathing suit like the one I was wearing. Knitting me swimsuits was another of her devices for saving my poor father money who, as she frequently pointed out, would have had to buy them otherwise at great expense. The aunts were all tightly corseted, even Aunty Mavis who was so slim she disappeared when she was sideways on. Grandma would have approved of the corsets but she would not have approved of their one concession to being by the seaside: their stockings were rolled neatly around their ankles exposing very white legs which, with their red and brown discolorations, and criss-crossed by the greeny-blue rivers of their varicose veins, resembled the maps we drew in geography.

I edged a little closer so that I could hear what Aunty Peggy was saying about Uncle Billy, but unfortunately my movement caught Aunty Betty's eye, and she remembered me.

'Remi, whatever are you doing in there?' she said. 'Come on, run along and play. You ought to be out enjoying yourself instead of moping in the corner.'

'I am enjoying myself Aunty. I don't want to go out there,' I said, eyeing the children. 'Everybody stares at me.'

'Nonsense, of course they don't,' Aunty Betty said, 'and

even if they do you must take no notice. I know, Uncle Theo can take you. Theo!' She shouted across to him.

Uncle Theo woke with a start and sat up. 'Yes dear,' he said.

'This child,' Aunty Betty said, pointing at me, 'is not getting any benefit sitting here in the corner. She says she is afraid to go out on her own, so you must take her to the water. The walk won't do you any harm either, you can't sleep your life away just because you're on holiday.'

The aunts nodded their approval; sighing, Uncle Theo looked enviously at the other uncles lightly snoring in their deckchairs, and took my hand.

'We'd better go,' he said, 'and get it over with.'

Reluctantly we set off on the long trek to the sea followed by the gawping children. We certainly made an interesting couple. With his white knotted bonnet, and his trousers rolled, Uncle Theo was a walking postcard in search of a caption, while my khaki and white knitted swimsuit was undoubtedly the only example of its kind probably in the world.

'Wool left over from the war, was it?' Aunty Madge had asked when she saw it.

'She doesn't need anything fancy at her age,' Aunty Betty had replied.

For my part I wished the suit had long sleeves and a hood, so icy was the wind from the sea as we headed down the beach.

Having dipped our toes in, and then quickly withdrawn them from the ripples of icy foam furrowing the sand, Uncle Theo and I stood shivering at the water's edge contemplating the distant horizon where the sky fell into the sea, when suddenly I was seized from behind, swept up and hurled into the waves. Gerald had crept up behind us unobserved. I clung to him screaming as he yelled with laughter and beat the water with his arms until it was a seething whirlpool around us. Screaming still, I pummelled his chest until he let me go, then scrambled back onto the beach and lay there winded, shaking the water out of my eyes and ears and hair, while the crowd of children danced around me gleefully.

Uncle Theo hurried to my aid, waving his fist at Gerald who was still cavorting in the sea, and helped me up.

'Come on, girl, we'd best get back, you'll catch your death else.' Gratefully I took his arm, my teeth chattering. 'You mustn't mind Gerald, he doesn't mean any harm, he's that daft he doesn't think what he's doing half the time.'

'No,' I said forlornly. How could I hold it against Gerald, I was in love with him.

We trudged back up the beach; my goose bumps felt as big as eggs. The wool of my bathing suit was completely waterlogged and filled up with sand, the crotch had sagged right down to my knees, and with every step our feet sank deeper into the mud which passed for sand at Mudeford-on-Sea.

'We're nearly there,' Uncle Theo said encouragingly.

I nodded, very nearly as miserable as I had ever been in my life.

It was just then that we were accosted by another holiday-maker coming in the opposite direction. He was large and friendly with a big round paunch and a great hairy chest; his black shorts reached to his knees which he raised high in the air as he ran. When he reached us he stopped, his hand irresistibly drawn to my hair, patted my head and said, 'What's the matter, sonny, this weather not hot enough for you, eh?'

I gave him a look of such ferocity that he withdrew his hand as if scalded, and I snarled, 'Can't you see I'm not a boy, I'm a girl, I'm wearing earrings, and I'm not a dog so don't pat me.'

'My,' said Uncle Theo admiringly, 'he won't do that again in a hurry.'

'No,' I said, ready to take on the world again.

In the second week the rain fell so solidly, it was as if we were looking at the world through sheets of cellophane; on the caravan site the sludge became waist-deep in places, and Mudeford appeared to be sliding back into the sea.

I was glad. The hot fug in the caravan was far preferable to the dreary cold of the beach, and no one could point and poke at me when the door was shut and we were safely inside.

Gerald was enraged at the rain which he took as a personal affront. I couldn't help thinking it served him right for throwing me so frequently into the sea; however many times it happened I was never prepared. He flailed around in the caravan like a huge bear in a trap and made life so intolerable, I took refuge with Aunty Madge and Uncle Reg in theirs, which they shared with Aunty Mavis and Uncle Alec. In the afternoon Aunty Madge sat up at the table in her blue dressing gown, and played Patience just as she did in Neasden. It was bliss to lie with my head in her lap rolling cigarettes one by one for Uncle Reg, snapping them out in smart precision like soldiers from the automatic roller in the top of his tobacco tin.

The air was thick with smoke which wound its way upwards in separate spirals and converged in a mushroom cloud against the ceiling before curling downwards again making Uncle Reg cough so violently that the whole caravan shook. Fatal for his chest, fatal, Aunty Madge said. Uncle Reg was as glad of the rain as I was, because indoors, mercifully, he was not obliged to put his teeth in. They crouched threateningly instead at the bottom of their glass of cleaning fluid like exotic creatures in an aquarium. Uncle Alec simply smoked. He was much admired as a snazzy dresser by Gerald, who loved his red braces and two-tone shoes, and so naturally I did too, but Uncle Alec never spoke, he merely smiled.

Of all Uncle Theo's sisters Aunty Mavis most resembled Aunty Moira, Bigmama; she had the same black hair and very white skin. There was nothing to choose between her and Margaret Lockwood, Aunty Madge said; they were as alike as two peas in a pod. Aunty Mavis sat across from Aunty Madge and painted and repainted her vermilion fingernails. In between she took long elegant drags from her cigarette. Her rollers stayed in her hair until supper when we all squashed around the table for fish and chips.

'I think Aunty Mavis is like Aunty Moira,' I said to Aunty Madge, from where I lay with my head on her lap.

'Yes, you're right there,' Aunty Madge said, squinting at her across the table. 'Both of them are as thin as rakes.'

'Moira never smoked a cigarette in her life,' Uncle Reg said as Aunty Mavis inhaled deeply.

'To look at, she means,' said Aunty Mavis, beginning on her third coat of nail polish. 'It's funny you saying that,' she said looking down at me, 'but I sometimes wonder what my life would have been like if I'd gone to Africa instead. Your grandfather asked me to dance first, you know.'

'I know,' I said. 'At the Hammersmith Palais, a well-known place for dancing.'

'He was a fine figure of a man,' Aunty Mavis said.

'Yes,' said Uncle Reg. 'Tall as a lamppost he was.'

'How is Moira anyway?' Aunty Mavis asked. 'She was over for some tests last time she was here, wasn't she? Is she OK now?'

'Oh yes, she's fine and whenever she writes she is still obsessed with that garden of hers,' Aunty Madge said with some asperity.

'A garden in Africa and I married Alec,' Aunty Mavis said, waving her nails playfully in the air towards Uncle Alec, who smiled back enigmatically through the smoke.

Suddenly, the caravan door flew open and Uncle Theo shot through the door which the wind banged shut behind him.

'Did I hear someone say Africa?' He shook the rain from his cap and before replacing it wiped his glistening pink head with a large spotted handkerchief. 'Anywhere's got to be better than this. It's like a bloody madhouse in there: every year Peg and Betty forget how much they hate each other, they come on holiday, it rains and they remember again. I don't know why we put ourselves through this.'

'Theo, watch your language in front of the child,' Aunty Madge scolded him.

'Beg your pardon. So that's where you are, move up.' Uncle Theo slipped into the seat beside me and lifted my legs onto his lap so that I was laid across both him and Aunty Madge.

'Yes,' I said, 'and there's nothing wrong with Africa either.'

'That's right, you stand up to him.'

'Don't you start, Madge, she doesn't need any urging from you, she can take care of herself. You should have seen the way she saw this fellow off on the beach. She fairly bit his head off.'

'Good for you, don't you take any nonsense from now on,' Aunty Madge said, shuffling her cards. 'It's about time.'

'You're right, it is, the poor kid's had a lot to put up with on that beach. We'll give them all a shock when the weather eases up. In future they're going to get as good as they give. Hey, is that the fish and chip van I can hear coming? Alec, come and help me out with these curlers.' Aunty Mavis hurried to the mirror.

With Aunty Madge and Aunty Mavis showing the way, we 'saw them off' triumphantly that year in Mudeford-on-Sea. Aunty Betty was right when she said they were putting ideas into my head and Gerald might not have joined in so enthusiastically had he known what the repercussions would be back home in Croydon.

A party of English explorers was trekking along a narrow jungle path in single file sandwiched between their African bearers. The African bearers were clearly nervous, the ones in front rolling their eyes fearfully and the ones bringing up the rear jumping out of their skins at every turn. The explorers, with not a hair out of place, were on their way to find Tarzan. He was the only one who knew the jungle well enough to lead them to the treasure, which, according to the map left by a previous explorer, was buried in a virtually inaccessible part of the jungle. It could only be reached by crossing impossible terrain inhabited by hostile natives and dangerous animals.

Suddenly up ahead, from the thick and impenetrable undergrowth, a terrifying thrashing and bellowing could be heard. The native bearers promptly downed their loads and disappeared to safety. I used to think that this was prudent behaviour on their part as they obviously knew the place and were familiar with the dangers and knew the best thing to do to avoid them. Now I bitterly resented their behaviour, because this kind of sensible precaution was considered cowardly in Croydon and, more to the point, the disapprobation rubbed off by association on me, the only representative of the black races in the whole of Thornton Heath.

The noise in the undergrowth reached a crescendo and one of the fleeing natives (you could depend on it every time) caught his foot in a tree root and fell heavily to the ground, rolling his eyes frantically and gibbering in fear. Whereupon the heroine, the only woman in the group, and who had previously shown no interest whatsoever in the bearers, unaccountably rushed to the native's assistance just as a huge, rampaging, mad bull elephant thundered through the dense vegetation into the clearing. The fallen native, galvanised into action by this terrifying sight, freed his foot and slunk off into the greenery with a hideous expression on his face, leaving the heroine to her fate. She, instead of running away, stood still, screaming, while the infuriated animal, ears flapping and trumpeting with all its might, lunged at her, determined to run her down. Certain death only seconds away, the hero came leaping to the heroine's defence and, with unerring aim, shot the elephant cleanly between the eyes, then dropped the gun in time to receive her fainting in his arms.

At that very moment, Tarzan burst onto the scene, calmed down the troupe of elephants who were following behind the mad bull and led the whole party off to the safety of his place for rest and recuperation before the next week.

Only one thing was certain and that was that the natives would not come out of it well. If there was danger, they could be relied upon to disgrace themselves and run away, leaving the hero and heroine and anyone else from England in the lurch, or else perish horribly. Considering that the jungle was their home, the natives were exasperatingly accident-prone. Hosts of them disappeared down the gullets of countless crocodiles, were crushed by rhinos, mauled by lions and strangled by snakes with no one to mourn their passing. My fate mirrored theirs in the games we played, I was thoroughly fed up with these celluloid Africans, ditto the Red Indians. They could carry on rolling their eyes and coming to grief week after week, but this African in Thornton Heath was going to do something about her situation.

'Gerald,' I said, as he was tying me up prior to lowering me into the snake pit at the side of the compost heap in Wilf's garden, 'why do you think it's always the natives who get eaten by the animals? After all, they've lived all their lives in the jungle, you'd think they'd have learnt a few tricks by now.'

'You would think so,' said Gerald. 'Maybe it's because they haven't got any guns.'

'I don't think that's the reason,' said Roger.

'Why do you think it is then?' Gerald asked him.

'I think it's because white people have got more brains,' said Roger.

'That's right,' agreed Doreen.

'Not all Africans are stupid,' I said indignantly, 'I've got just as much brains as you have.'

'It's only in the films,' Wilf said.

'Yeah, they're only stories,' said Paula. 'Are we going to get on with this game or what? If you don't hurry up and finish tying her up, Gerald, I'll get cramp in my leg waiting to be rescued here forever.' Paula tossed her long blonde hair.

I could see that reasoning wasn't going to change things. I would have to try something else.

'Wilf,' I said, 'I think it's very unfair that you always get the smallest parts to play.'

'Elephants and rhinos aren't small.'

'You know what I mean.'

'Yeah, I suppose so.'

'Just because you're the smallest and I'm the youngest we get the worst.'

'I don't see how we can go against Gerald.'

'We could play other games.'

'What other games?'

'King Arthur and his Knights of the Round Table for instance.'

'Uh huh.'

'It'd be more fun to play a knight than an animal or a native.'

'Might be.'

I left him to think about it. He wasn't persuaded in a day but eventually he agreed. We laid our plans in secret and when the occasion arrived we were ready.

'Remi,' Gerald shouted, 'off we go, put the baggage on your head and lead on.'

'I'm not carrying it on my head,' I said.

'Oh all right, carry it anywhere you like, but lead on.'

As I led on down the narrow alleyway and pushed open the gate into Roger's garden, in the dense undergrowth beyond the hedge the pawing and thumping of some mighty animal could be heard. The noise reverberated like thunder through the jungle, and sure enough Wilf came charging around the hedge bellowing and raging, straight towards the native bearer, who, with what I hoped was unimpeachable dignity, laid down the luggage, and with unerring aim struck the rhino just above the horn. With equal dignity the rhino buckled to the ground beneath the astonished gaze of the explorers.

'What do you think you're doing?' yelled Gerald.

'I have killed him with my spear,' I said.

'What spear, you haven't got a spear,' Doreen said.

'Natives usually carry spears,' said the rhino from the ground.

'As for you, what did you fall down for?' Gerald said furiously. 'Get up and shut up.'

Wilf arose and came to stand beside me. 'We have decided,' he said, 'that we're not going to play these silly games any more. She,' he said, nodding his head at me as I stepped closer to him, 'is fed up with being a native all the time and as for me I only ever get to play animals or Red Indians. I'm fed up too. You can play by yourselves.'

Our knees quaking, we passed through the gate and out of Roger's garden.

Gerald was unforgiving. I took to following Uncle Theo around instead, working beside him on the allotment, carefully weeding the little section he set aside especially for me. I strongly suspected that Uncle Theo carried out secret work on my bit because it always looked healthy and flourishing when I arrived for the holiday, and kind of wilted and dead by the time I returned to school having forbidden Uncle Theo to lay a finger on it during the time I was at home.

'Uncle Theo, do you think of me as a darkie?' I asked him.

'No, of course not, I think of you like any other child, like my granddaughter.'

'You really don't think of me as a darkie?'

'No, I do not,' he said, carefully raking the soil around his leeks.

'Doreen says I'm a darkie and that English people don't like darkies.'

'She's just talking daft. Sensible people don't think that way, as far as they're concerned people are people, they like them for what they are.'

'What am I then?'

'Like I said, you're a child, quite a nice child for most of the time.'

'What will I be when I grow up?'

'You'll be an African, a coloured person.'

'Why a coloured person?'

'Because, I suppose, you're not white,' Uncle Theo said.

I studied him carefully as he turned back to his raking. His skin was scarlet from the sun, his eyes were emerald green and his little pointed teeth were green too.

I thought, Grandma would have said this man is talking nonsense. Mind you, it was becoming increasingly difficult to imagine what Grandma would have said. I was beginning to think that she and Aunt Rose and Patience and Alaba were all figments of my imagination.

Wilf and I met by the lamppost outside his gate. He said he thought that if Gerald and the gang continued to ignore us we might have to revise our position, which was that they needed us more than we needed them. I reassured him that though Gerald was a great man of action – he could jump on and off trams when they were moving, wangle us into the cinema or the swimming pool without paying and melt the ice at Streatham Ice Rink with the power of his blades – he was very short on imagination; he depended on Wilf and me – they all did, I pointed out – for the refinements which we supplied in our games. We'd all be back together soon, I predicted. I was confident because Gerald depended on me for something else that Wilf knew nothing about. I read to Gerald every night before I went to bed. He loved stories but, as Aunty Betty said, though he could manage the *Dandy* and the *Beano*, he was no reader. We had stopped at a particularly exciting point in *Treasure Island* and I knew he was longing to get back to it.

'So you reckon we should hang on a bit longer?' Wilf said.

'Yes, I think so,' I replied and hurried in because I had promised to help Maureen prepare for her works annual summer dance. I was grateful to have something to do. I had exhausted all of Gerald's comics which lined his den in the air raid shelter from floor to ceiling and I must admit I found them all the more enjoyable because they were banned at Chilcott Manor. For the life of me I could not imagine why.

Maureen was twenty-one and she was afraid of being left on the shelf, but, as I admired her image in the looking-glass, I did not think it would be for long and I told her so.

'Oh, Remi,' she said, flushing, 'you're just saying that.'

'No, honestly,' I said. However, it was a lucky thing that she didn't take after Aunty Betty; although she was tall, she was willowy and dark-haired, like Aunty Mavis and Aunty Moira. And she really was quite pretty when she took her glasses off.

There were six yards of tulle in Maureen's frock, Aunty Betty said, and I believed her. Her stole was dusted with sequins which sparkled like stars. Maureen said she was afraid she wouldn't be able to see without her glasses, but Aunty Betty wouldn't hear of her wearing them. She too was afraid that Maureen might be left on the shelf. When Tony, her boyfriend, sounded his horn outside, Maureen bumped into the door jamb trying to get out but Aunty Betty kept a firm hold of her glasses, and she had to make the best of it without them.

We helped her manoeuvre her skirt sideways through the door and feel her way downstairs before I rushed, and Aunty Betty followed as fast as she could, to the front bedroom to catch a glimpse of Tony who was having a big problem squashing Maureen into the side car of his motorcycle before whisking her off. Aunty Betty had very high hopes of Tony for Maureen. Paula from next door said that her mother was sick to death of hearing what a nice family he came from and how his brother was at university. I had my fingers crossed for Maureen too, but none of this compared with playing games in the alley and across the gardens.

At breakfast the next morning Gerald told me ever so casually to be sure to be ready to accompany him as usual to Saturday morning pictures. He said it between shovelling in mouthfuls of porridge; winter or summer, it made no difference, Gerald began the day with a saucepan of porridge. I took my time walking out of the room but once outside the door I raced up the stairs to prepare. I was debating whether to dab on some 'Evening in Paris' to celebrate the occasion when Maureen, who had come home late from her dance and was still in bed, suddenly sat up, stared at me for a second and then slammed back down again on her back like a piece of felled timber. She looked as if she were dead, but I decided not to risk taking the scent all the same and brushed my hair instead.

We called in on Wilf on the way to the cinema. He was so happy he didn't look where he was going and was nearly run over when we were crossing the road all strung out in a long line. Roger only just managed to haul him back in time.

Walking back home, Gerald, again ever so casually, said that maybe we should think of some new games to play. I put forward King Arthur and his Knights of the Round Table which I was reading at school and Wilf suggested Martians from Outer Space. He and I both knew that he would never be King Arthur but he could be a knight which all the books said was a noble thing to be, and, as for Martians, well there was no reason for Doreen to look in my direction. Martians, as everybody knew, were green.

– Chapter 8 –

'Gerald,' I asked, 'what really made you change your mind about the Tarzan games?'

'It was something Aunty Mavis said at Mudeford, wasn't it?'

'What was that?'

'She said you was as English as the rest of us now. I mean what do you know about Africa? You've been here as long as you been there. You're not a savage any more, it's simple.'

'I know, but I do remember what it was like when I was there and it wasn't like Tarzan or how the mistresses at school say it is.'

'Are they giving you grief then?'

'Yes, they're just like the films, saying horrid things about Africa. I don't have a problem with the girls any more.'

'I dunno why that is, with the teachers I mean.'

'I dunno either,' I said.

We were both contemplative for a moment.

'Maybe . . . you should knock their blocks off as well, like I suggested before with the girls.'

'Maybe,' I said.

Gerald would have been perfect as Henry the Eighth, I thought.

What he would actually have liked to be, of course, was a fighter pilot and, in order to strengthen my resolve, should I decide to follow his advice and 'knock a few blocks off', he gave me one of his prized Battle of Britain Spitfires, which, he said, was also a late eleventh birthday present and a reward for reading *Treasure Island* (at least ten times by my reckoning) aloud to him.

I thought the aeroplane would have been even more beautiful painted blue all over instead of just on the underneath. Gerald very nearly took it back when I pointed this out to him. He said that it was camouflaged so that the enemy looking up at it would think it was part of the sky, but looking down on it they would imagine, because of its green mottled top and sides, that it was a bush. What I wanted to know was why you would have a bush flying around in the sky. Of course I didn't say so, and in fact when I arrived back at school the camouflage worked very well against the counterpane between my pyjama case and my boxing kangaroo. Gerald would have been disappointed to learn that, upon reflection, and especially in view of my father's continuing strictures on my bad behaviour, I resolved to hang up my boxing gloves and adopt aeroplane camouflage instead. This was not the inspiration he'd intended, but even Gerald might have had a problem knocking the block off Chilcott Manor. Besides, as Aunty Mavis said, I was English now.

'I am going to keep out of trouble this year!' I announced grandly to Jessica, Anita, Sarah and Minnie. 'When my father opens my next school report, he will be in for a shock. From now on I am going to behave as Miss Bowles says I should, as a perfect ambassador for my race. Except, of course, that I am English now.'

'What do you mean you're English now?' Anita demanded.

'I've been in England as long as I was in Africa practically, that's why.'

'We've been trying to tell you that for ages,' Jessica said.

'Why the sudden change? Would you like a sausage? I saved some from supper yesterday.' Sarah broke the cold burnt offerings in half and distributed them.

'Yes, what about the honour of Africa?' Minnie said through her mouthful of sausage.

'Oh that,' I said casually. 'Africa will just have to manage without me.'

'Miss Flood will be pleased at any rate to have you off the blue bench and back on the games teams,' Jessica laughed.

'Now that you're so English,' Anita said, looking round at the others. 'I'm sure you won't mind auditioning for the choir like everyone else.'

There was an embarrassed silence.

'What do you mean?' I asked her suspiciously.

'I mean you're the only one in the Junior School Choir who was given a place without an audition. We think it's unfair and you should be tested.'

'Who's we?'

'Everyone in the choir,' Anita said.

The other three remained silent.

'Is that true?' I appealed to them.

'Yes,' Minnie acknowledged reluctantly.

'Why now suddenly?'

'Because most of us will be moving up into the Senior School next year and this will be our last chance to win the cup.'

'So?'

'So you can't sing. You'll ruin our chances, you always do. Everybody knows that.' Anita was vehement.

'Miss Sweetwood doesn't. She's the singing mistress and she put me in the choir.' I remained unconvinced.

'It would be the same if Miss Flood put me in the netball team,' Anita said.

'My goodness, as bad as that?' Everyone knew Anita couldn't hit or catch a ball to save her life.

'You're always saying you don't want special treatment,' she retorted furiously, her face as red as her plaits, 'now's the time to prove it.'

Wounded, I finally agreed. It was an undeniable fact that Miss Sweetwood had put me in the choir without a test, because, as she put it, 'You people from Africa all have lovely voices: look at Paul Robeson.' I must say I was delighted to be in the choir and I was very grateful to Mr Robeson, whoever he was, especially as my piano teacher, Miss Byngham, had told me I was tone deaf.

After testing me, Miss Sweetwood sat down heavily on the piano stool; long strands of her hair fell loose from the bun on top of her head giving her a wild, dishevelled look.

'How strange,' she said, looking at me perplexed. 'How very strange.'

'What is strange, Miss Sweetwood?' I asked.

'You can't sing,' she said, 'you cannot sing at all.'

'No?' I said, not entirely surprised.

'No,' she said with a sigh.

'Then why did you put me in the choir?' I asked her.

Miss Sweetwood looked at me accusingly. 'I assumed you would have a beautiful voice like Paul Robeson, like all your people.'

'Who is this Paul Robeson?'

'He is an American; a truly great singer.'

'But I'm not an American,' I said. 'I'm from Nigeria.'

'Ah, but he is a Negro!' said Miss Sweetwood triumphantly.

'Ah, yes of course!' I agreed, still completely in the dark.

'Well, how did it go?' Jessica asked anxiously on my return.

'It's official,' I replied bitterly, 'I can't sing.'

I regretted no longer being able to enjoy the kudos of being in the choir as the annual music and drama festival drew near, but there were plenty of other events in the drama section, for which I was entered, and the relief I felt at being treated in the same way as everybody else was immeasurably sweeter. Indeed so keen was I now not to be regarded as different from everyone else, I made no demur when in a discussion with Miss Miles during a history lesson on the slave trade, Heidi Goodchild said it had been authoritatively proved that Africans had smaller brains, and I remained perfectly silent when Mr Stephens, a missionary visiting from Africa, told all of us in the Junior School in his talk that Africans were like children in real need of the guidance that Europeans could give them. Miss Liddel, our geography mistress, introducing Mr Stephens, said she would like us to welcome him warmly for he had worked with Albert Schweitzer, no less, a great man. We all assumed, correctly, that she meant Mr Schweitzer, but she clearly had a great regard for Mr Stephens too. After all, I thought, it was quite possible that Mr Stephens had met and worked with completely different Africans, of a kind I had never met. And this was what I told Anita when she tackled me on my silence afterwards.

Miss Clifford-Broughton said she would not be at all surprised if I walked away with the Poetry-Speaking Prize this year and Miss Flood said that her only dilemma concerning our almost certain victory over St Esmeralda's, our arch rivals in netball, was whether to switch me from centre court to defence where I was equally valuable. Miss Valentine said that netball was only a game and that whereas we were never likely to set foot on a playing field again once we were adults, mathematics would stand us in good stead for the rest of our lives. She personally could not understand all this hysteria over a ball game.

Miss Valentine and I had never solved the problem between us, she frequently told me how much she disliked me, and Anita had overheard her telling Miss Miles, shortly after one of the numerous occasions she had sent me out of her class to sit on the blue bench, that there was something about me which made her see red. I disliked her equally, and I was no longer afraid of her: she was not, five years on, the terrifying figure I had first encountered in the gloom of the drawing room on only my fourth day in England. Nevertheless it was odd that although Miss Valentine so disliked me, she insisted I sit next to her at lunch whenever she was at the head of my table. Our head mistress enjoyed intelligent conversation, she said, and most of the girls in the Junior School were too frightened of her to be able to supply it. Often she made me change places in the middle of the meal. I was never lost for words, she said, banishing the tongue-tied offender from her side to the bottom of the table.

Steely fresh in an iron-grey costume, Miss Valentine sat straight-backed as ever behind the table on the platform, having set us to calculate how long it would take six workmen working at a certain speed to dig a specified length of ditch. Instead of pondering this problem my mind fixed itself instead on the dilemma confronting Miss Flood and drifted irretrievably out through the leaded window panes towards the netball court from where it was suddenly and sharply recalled.

'As you are looking out of the window, Remi, I take it you have solved the problem?'

'Er, yes, Miss Valentine,' I replied.

'What is the answer?'

'Two days,' I guessed wildly.

Silence fell over the form room.

'How did you arrive at this figure?'

I guessed wildly again and the silence lengthened.

Then Miss Valentine said, 'I see you have not been paying attention. This was a perfectly simple problem which even an African savage could have solved. Sit down, I shall speak to you after the lesson.'

In a flash I forgot my resolve and all about aeroplane camouflage markings.

'Africans are not savages, Miss Valentine.'

Miss Valentine strode down from the platform, snatched me by the arm, marched me from the room, out of the school building and down the drive, not stopping until she had thrust me violently out of the gate. I was not fit, she said, to be in the school, and she left me speechless outside on the road. I leant against the high brick wall and it was as it had been in Liverpool all those years ago when I realised that my mother and Grandma and Patience were back home in Africa and I was alone in England. Not knowing what else to do I stayed where I was until Miss Bowles came to fetch me. Miss Valentine apologised for putting me out of the gate, she said. Something within her had snapped. Notwithstanding, she said, for answering back in that fashion I must forfeit my place in the forthcoming netball match. Minnie said that Miss Flood was even more upset than me at this, which was probably true, she certainly shed tears when we lost to St Esmeralda's. And as Sarah pointed out, Miss Flood didn't have the compensation of winning the Poetry-Speaking Prize, which Miss Clifford-Broughton said was due not only to my perfect diction but also to a certain warm quality in my dark brown African voice. The Junior School Choir won the cup in the music competition but, as Jessica said, it was probably coincidence and had nothing whatsoever to do with my absence from its ranks.

My father received no surprises after all when he opened my next school report. Miss Bowles having informed him that his daughter was behaving on occasion like a wild animal, he wrote back furiously that he had sent me to England to become a young lady and instead I appeared to be turning into a baboon. I must have got into the wrong set, he said, and advised me to change my associates.

'How unkind,' Anita said, when she saw what he had written. 'However I comfort myself that at least I know how to eat a banana correctly, with the appropriate knife and fork.'

So it was with trepidation that I opened a second letter in the middle of term. My friends were equally curious to learn what stupendous occurrence had prompted this break with tradition.

'Quickly,' Anita said, shaking my arm, 'tell us what he says.'

' "You will be pleased to hear," ' I read out, ' "that your mother and I together with the rest of the family will be arriving shortly in the UK. I shall visit you at school before the term is out." '

'My goodness,' said Jessica, 'that's wonderful news.'

'Yes,' I said, at a loss for words.

'But it will be rather peculiar,' Minnie said, 'after all this time, won't it?'

'I can't imagine it,' I said, and the five of us including Sarah, who had said nothing, sat silently, imagining.

That night I lay awake in the dark and tried to conjure up the faces of my parents. My mother's image was undimmed, burnished and sharp as the high curves of her cheeks, but my father's hovered stubbornly at the back of my mind, and would not be summoned. Rummaging further I found my baby brother, who, of course, was not a baby now, with his big head and big eyes, smiling; and I fell asleep with his picture held fast in my mind. For a while the imminent arrival of my parents occupied my thoughts, and my lack of concentration nearly cost me my place on the rounders team, but by and by, the flawless summer days resumed their rhythm and I forgot for a week at a time.

'Remi, Remi.' I heard my name being called. It was the eve of the senior tennis tournament, and Jessica and I prised our gaze from the practice game between our idols, Barbara McKenzie and Lizzie Browne. 'Miss Bowles wants you,' the little first-form messenger blurted out.

'Thank you,' I said.

As she turned and trotted off again, Jessica said at once, 'What have you done?'

'Nothing as far as I know,' I said.

Miss Bowles was waiting for me in the hall, and through the open doorway I could see that she was unusually animated, her white candlewax cheeks were aflame, and she was gliding restlessly to and fro across the flagstones.

'Ah, there you are,' she said, seizing my arm. Her voice had lost all its sibilant softness. I concluded that I must have done something very serious indeed to render Miss Bowles to this state, but I couldn't for the life of me think what it could be. I had been on my best behaviour pending the tennis tournament.

'You have some visitors,' she said.

Good heavens was that all, I thought, and my heart, which had been hammering in anticipation of disaster, all the way from the tennis courts, slowed down to normal.

'In the drawing room, come with me,' Miss Bowles said, and keeping hold of my arm, shepherded me quickly across the hall and flung open the door.

'Here she is,' she announced to the room, and then pushing me forward she whispered loudly in my ear, 'your father has come to see you.'

And my heart, which had slowed down to normal, stopped.

The room was dark except for thick wedges of sunlight which slanted in through the leaded windows and gathered in silver pools on the floor. A mile away two tall figures stood in silhouette, their features indistinguishable against the light. My feet had taken root by the door; I could feel the roots digging deep and spreading out under the floor in such a way that unless I moved now I would not be able to move again.

Nerving myself, I made my way across the room, cutting

briskly through the shadows and the pools of sunlight until I reached them and their faces which were wavering slightly, as if I were seeing them through water, came at last into focus. They watched me approach in silence and gravely, in silence, we studied each other. Then I put out my hand and looking from one to the other said brightly in my best English, 'How do you do, which one of you is my father?'

A look of extreme shock registered on both their faces. The figure on my right sank down rather abruptly on the sofa, followed almost immediately by the other, who, having said hallo, sat down heavily beside him.

I placed myself on an armchair opposite and waited politely, without breathing.

'I am your father,' said my father indignantly, 'and this is your Uncle Yomi.'

'Ah, how do you do,' I said, jumping up to shake hands again.

'I beg you spare me,' said my father, 'do not say, "How do you do" one more time. Do you not remember me at all?'

'No,' I said.

'Oh my God,' said my father.

'You have grown very tall,' my Uncle Yomi said.

'Tall!' said my father. 'The child has grown into a giantess. Come and kiss me.'

I jumped up a second time and my father enveloped me in a bear hug. Then he held me at arm's length so he could look at me. He told me that my mother sent me her love and that the other children were mad with excitement at the prospect of seeing their big sister about whom they had heard so much.

If I had passed my father in the street, I would not have recognised him. I remembered nothing of his appearance except that he was tall. He was still tall. Used now to white skins, he and Uncle Yomi appeared jet black to me; surreptitiously, I looked down at my own arms comparing; yes, I was not far off in colour. Suddenly I felt reassured.

'Please give my love to Mummy too,' I said.

'What about your sisters?' my father asked. 'Shall I give them your love too?'

'Well I don't know them,' I said doubtfully, 'but, yes, I suppose you could.'

My father burst into laughter; he laughed with his whole body, throwing back his head against the sofa, shaking his shoulders and stamping his feet. Uncle Yomi joined in and so did I, although I had no idea why they were laughing.

I laughed because now I remembered: I remembered my father chasing Baba Cook; I remembered spying on him dancing with my mother on the veranda at Enugu; I remembered Sisi Bola's wedding. We could have been in Africa, I had not heard this kind of laughter since I'd left.

'She has become an Englishwoman,' my father said.

They were still laughing when the maid came in with the tea tray and put it down on the table beside me; there were cucumber sandwiches, buttered scones, strawberry jam and cake.

'Do you take milk, Daddy?' I asked him as I poured the tea.

'Would you like some sugar, Uncle Yomi? Do have some cake,' I said and pressed a slice on him.

As I presided grandly over the teacups and passed the plates, showing off in front of my visitors, who stared in disbelief, I could not help reflecting that this was the very drawing room where, six years old and newly arrived from Africa, I had sat hypnotised by fear under the gimlet eye of Miss Valentine, and then, unaccustomed as I was to using a cake fork, had scattered this same Madeira cake in a fine shower all over the Turkey carpet.

'The transformation has been too complete,' said Uncle Yomi.

'I think so,' said my father, mopping his eyes.

But they would never know what it had cost me.

– Chapter 9 –

'She's a beautiful woman, your mother,' Aunty Madge said, 'and she's a lovely person too.'

'Is she?' I said. 'I wouldn't know, would I?' I looked sideways at Aunty Madge while running my finger around the inside of her mixing bowl. She was making something soft and spongy for Uncle Reg's tea, and something for us as well, she said. It tasted delicious so far.

'Well you mustn't miss the opportunity to get to know her now.' Aunty Madge looked me straight in the eye. 'She's very anxious to get to know you again. Sitting right there where you are, she told me not a single day went by since you left, that she didn't think about you, and wonder how you were getting on.'

'Did she really say that, Aunty?'

'Yes, she did.'

'Cross your heart and hope to die?'

'On my honour,' Aunty Madge said, brushing and blowing off the flour, and turning her kitchen into a snow storm. 'I can't see a thing now, pass me a towel, there, behind the door so I can wipe my glasses.'

The kitchen door was open on the garden, it was a warm day and the bees were busy, but they appeared to be avoiding, with good reason I thought, Uncle Reg's electric pink hydrangeas. Mentally I willed the bees over the hedge into the next door garden where I could hear my sisters playing and briefly imagined their laughter turning to shrieks of alarm as they were swarmed. My father had rented the house next door to Uncle Reg and Aunty Madge in Neasden for the period of his leave.

'You can't imagine what it's like next door,' I said, sitting down. 'My mother has no idea how to keep house. I think I'll come and stay here with you. She doesn't know how to cook either.' I dipped my finger into the mixing bowl again.

'Stop that this minute, you hear me, and take your finger out of there!' Aunty Madge crammed her glasses back on her nose and slapped my hand away.

'You should be with her right now seeing what you could do to help instead of shooting your mouth off here. What do you know about it? That poor woman has been waited on hand and foot since the day she was born, and now suddenly, here she is in a foreign country expected to cook and clean and wash for a large household, look after her husband and cope with five children, and the eldest one she hasn't even seen for six years.'

'It's not my fault,' I said, aggrieved.

'I know, I know, but it wasn't easy for her either you being away, and it's not easy for her now. She has a lot on her plate.' Aunty Madge pummelled her cake mixture. 'And your father's no help!' She whacked it again with her wooden spoon.

That was true. On the one occasion he'd done the shopping, as he did not approve of paying for carrier bags, he had taken a luggage hold-all with him, and returned with it full of Brussels sprouts. When Aunty Madge had asked him why, he had said it was her fault because she had failed to state on her list the number of pounds he should buy.

'I didn't put Brussels sprouts on the list,' Aunty Madge said.

'You see!' said my father. 'And I needed them to eat with my steak.'

'What steak?' my mother asked.

'I did not buy any,' he said, 'there was not enough room in the bag.' And he stalked out of the room with ineffable dignity.

Watching him go, my mother told Aunty Madge she was in a state of shock. Life in England was not at all what she had been led to believe. All the time she was growing up Aunty Moira had given her the impression that England was

133

paradise on earth, which my father's and Aunt Harriet's descriptions of their student days had done nothing to dispel. She had understood from Aunty Moira that everyone in England had servants just like at home. That was before the war, Aunty Madge said, things were very different now. And anyway she couldn't think how Moira could have given that impression, there had never been any servants in their family that she knew of. If it hadn't been for Aunty Madge, my mother said, she didn't know what she would have done.

I didn't know what I would have done without Aunty Madge either and that was why I was spending most of my time in her house. I was very disappointed in my brother, he wasn't at all how I remembered him. He was nearly as big as me now and we fought over everything. He was the boy, he said; but I was the eldest, I maintained. My sisters were no better – They were just spoilt, my mother played with them all the time. Aduke was tall and skinny like me, she had a round face with a permanently serious expression and most of the time she was as distant as a cloud. Yejide was the image of my mother, Aunty Madge said, and she clung to her like a burr, terrified of everything in England. And who could blame her? Uncle Reg said when I told him. She was the one strangers cooed over. Yinka the youngest was plump and genial, she would go to anyone who offered her food, my mother said. She was also brave; she didn't scream when she fell off the neighbour's garage roof and gashed her leg open on some corrugated iron, she bit on the towel and let me do my best with TCP and bandages. When my mother discovered the wound and called the doctor, he said my sister should have had half a dozen stitches and would carry the scar to her dying day. Aunty Madge said the poor baby could have died, which was true given how rusty the iron was, but Aunty Madge didn't know that. My mother, who had forbidden us the garage roof, said that I was no help to her at all, which was also true.

Aunty Madge made a cup of tea after the doctor had left and my mother said she despaired of ever being able to cope. She should not be downhearted, she was learning fast, Aunty

Madge said. She could now operate the Hoover, and she could go shopping by herself. I laughed aloud at this and my mother rounded on me swiftly.

'As for you,' she said, 'what can you do? Nothing. And look how long you have been in England.'

'I can ballet dance,' I said, 'and country dance, and I can sit a horse nicely.'

Aunty Madge looked at me and choked on her cigarette, while my mother, laughing too, smacked her vigorously on the back.

'Those accomplishments will stand you in good stead one day, I'm sure,' Aunty Madge said between gasps, 'but they're not much use to your mother at the present time.'

'And another thing,' my mother said when she had recovered, 'why when I go out do people ask if I am Jamaican?'

Alas I could not help her there either.

My father inhabited a different plane from the rest of us, said Aunty Madge. He was sublimely unaware, she said, of the monumental adjustments going on around him. This, my mother told her, was because at home, in Nigeria, where he was now a High Court Judge, he never had to deal with practical matters. Outside his house he was protected by his office, and inside by herself and the servants. Uncle Reg's mouth dropped open and his teeth would have fallen out, had he had them in, as my mother explained that if my father wanted to use the telephone, for example, someone else dialled the number for him and held the receiver, and only when the other person had come on the line was the receiver handed to my father to speak into. That explained why, Aunty Madge said, he appeared as innocent as a newborn babe. My father was very upset. This was untrue, he said, and in fact one of the satisfactions for him in coming to England was to be able to rough it like the next man in the street. Aunty Madge replied that it was my mother who was actually roughing it. My father did not appear to hear.

In practice he behaved exactly as he did in Nigeria. He ordered people to help him, and most of them were so taken by surprise that they did as he asked. He was known in

Neasden, not entirely sarcastically, Uncle Reg said, as his Lordship. Shopkeepers who did not normally deliver could often be seen toiling up the High Street behind him bearing some heavy purchase, which obviously he could not carry. The sight tickled him pink, Uncle Reg said. My father was tickled too, he was delighted to be back in England, rediscovering his favourite city and renewing old acquaintances from his university and law school days twenty years before. Why, twenty years was nothing, he said, it seemed like only yesterday. Twenty years was a lifetime, my mother said. At which my father pointed out that there were twenty years between them. I meant only in certain situations, my mother quickly corrected herself, glancing sideways at Aunty Madge. When it transpired that my father's idea of roughing it was travelling on public transport, Uncle Reg said that he could not recommend it too highly as a method of experiencing life as it was really lived in England. Uncle Reg, Aunty Madge told my mother later, had just that very summer been promoted to Inspector on the buses.

One morning, wearing a cardigan and slippers, my father went out and did not come back. Depend on it, I said, he was out there making contact with the next man in the street. My mother was sure he had a perfectly good reason, he had merely forgotten to tell us what it was. My sister Aduke said that our father was like Macavity the mystery cat, never there.

'Why don't you sleep with me tonight, Remi?' my mother said.

I lay in bed and watched her seated at the dressing table plaiting her hair up ready for the night. I had imagined our reunion frequently since coming to England and I had always imagined our meeting taking place in Grandpa's house, as when in the past she and my father had come up to Lagos to visit. We would be either in her room, with the blue and white Indian coverlet on the big double bed and the shaded balconies overlooking the street, or in the coolness of Grandma's sitting room with the rocking chair in front of the tallboy, where, no matter what, because of all the traffic through the room, the rugs were always askew on the polished floor. I had not imagined a house in Neasden.

My mother was smaller than I remembered – we were both very nearly the same height now – but apart from that she hadn't changed a bit; she looked young, nothing like the mothers of my friends at school. In fact she did not seem like a grown-up at all. In this setting, she appeared as exotic as a bird of paradise set down on Uncle Theo's allotment.

Addressing my image reflected in the oval looking glass in the centre of the dressing table, my mother told me my father had decided that I should change schools. He was not satisfied with the academic standard at Chilcott Manor. I was not entirely surprised; he'd been hinting at this possibility for some time. I would miss Jessica. Where was I going? I asked. Somewhere in the Midlands, my mother said, Dove House School was the name, if she remembered correctly, and it was sister to the one my father had chosen for my brother Tunji.

'I do hope you will be happy there,' my mother said, climbing into bed.

'I feel sorry for Tunji.' I moved over to make room.

'Why, what will happen to him?' she asked anxiously.

'It will be worse for him because he's a boy. My friend Anita says that boys are subjected to horrible tortures when they first start school: her brother was practically killed,' I said darkly.

'Tell me, what kind of things did they do to you?'

'You cannot imagine!'

'I think I can.'

'Oh no, you can't.'

'Try me.'

'It was terrible, you know. Bigmama lied to me. She told me that you would be waiting in Liverpool, and Grandma and Patience. You weren't there.'

'We would have been if we could,' my mother said.

'Hmm! Well you weren't.'

'I know and I am very sorry. What happened when you arrived at school?'

'I thought the mistresses were witches, I thought they were going to eat me up when Aunt Grace left me. They made me sleep in this huge freezing dormitory all by myself in the dark, with the window wide open for any monster to fly in, every night for a week before the other girls arrived.' My mother had tears in her eyes, I noted with satisfaction.

'And then when the girls did come back they wouldn't come near me because they said the black came off.'

'How long was that for?'

'A whole year.'

'But they came round in the end?' My mother wiped her eyes with her handkerchief.

'Yes,' I said. 'The French mistress told them,' and I leapt out of bed to show her how Anita had stood up that first night, with her red hair blazing under the light, like Queen Boadicea in her chariot, and then how I had turned the tables on her. It sounded suspiciously as if my mother were laughing now.

'It was not funny,' I said, 'I found out I knew nothing about Africa and I had to make up stories about life in the jungle.'

'Life in the jungle?'

'Yes. I took all the stories from the Tarzan films at Saturday morning pictures in Croydon. I told them my daddy was a Chief and that we all wore leopard skins and ate snake stew sitting around the fire in our village.'

'Oh my God! I want to see Grandma's face when she hears that one.' My mother wiped her eyes again.

'Miss Clifford-Broughton didn't approve of Croydon either,' I continued. 'She thought people spoke worse English there than in Lagos. At first, when I asked her why de cow was brown in the exercise she gave me, she said' – here I threw my head back, putting on Miss Clifford-Broughton's voice – 'the colour of the cow is unimportant, what you have to remember, Remi, is to say "the" not "de". But then when I came back after the holidays' – here I changed to Aunty Betty's voice – 'with 'ow now brown cow, Miss Clifford-Broughton changed her mind.'

'Stop. Stop!' My mother was convulsed on the bed. 'I have a stitch in my side.'

I jumped back on the bed beside her and she hugged me close.

'You know,' she said, serious again, 'when you left, it was

138

as if a piece of me had been wrenched away. You are a very special child.'

'You bet!' I said.

We were laughing when we fell asleep.

My father returned, after three days. He had been to Germany to collect an antique clock for his collection at home.

'Remi,' he announced, 'I have found you another school.'

'In Germany?' I feigned alarm.

'Have no fear, you will be very close to your brother at his school; he will look after you. I took him to inspect his school before you broke up for the holidays, now it's your turn.'

My father had decided to remove me from my school because, unimpeachable as it was in certain respects – my general demeanour and my French accent, for example, were excellent – for the purposes of my future life (helping to build Nigeria), university and a profession such as law or medicine would be more appropriate than a finishing school, the destination of the majority of pupils at Chilcott Manor. I would miss my friends, I said. I would make new ones, my father said.

Dove House School was not as large or as imposing as Chilcott Manor. It lay secluded behind a modest driveway on the outskirts of the little market town of Worcester. The Georgian façade was ivy-covered and drenched in sunlight which turned the scalloped leaves into shiny green scales and dripped from them like water. Miss Bellamy, the head-mistress, greeted us in the black and white tiled hall and suggested that we tour the grounds first. Smooth lawns and ordered flowerbeds lay contentedly within mellow brick walls, on their best behaviour in the summer sun, but I wondered grimly how they would look in winter. My father, who would not be there in the winter, was quite seduced.

In the drawing room after tea, Miss Bellamy, brisk and efficient in navy blue, was not visibly impressed when I told her that at my last school I had learned, among other things, to darn, knit and sew, embroider and keep accounts, and not least to prepare junket for an invalid. She replied, 'Here, as you have seen, we have a science laboratory, and we place particular emphasis in the curriculum on physics and mathematics. You will also be taught Latin and Greek.'

My father listened, entranced; I was unimpressed. I had not been intimidated by the science laboratory, and I was not afraid of Latin or Greek. My only feeling was regret at having to change from a lacrosse to a hockey stick. This school will be a breeze, I thought.

Now that the business was over, my father said, we could have some fun, before he left he wanted us all to meet his friends. 'Why?' we asked suspiciously. You will see, he mysteriously replied. My mother washed and pressed us all and put ribbons in our hair, except of course for my brother, and we were ready long before my father, who had said that absolutely on no account should we be late. As his contribution towards helping my mother, he had volunteered to clean his own shoes, and this operation was taking longer than he had anticipated and longer than had been prescribed by the *Encyclopaedia Britannica*, or in whatever manual my mother reckoned he had looked up shoe cleaning. Although my father had enveloped himself and large portions of the room in dust sheets, he still managed to get polish on the portions he'd left uncovered.

We set off at last, all seven of us, down the street to the bus stop, with my father in charge in front because he was the one who knew London. As a family we were an attractive but unfamiliar sight in London in 1953. Walking along, we tried to emulate my father's apparent indifference to the open-mouthed stares which followed us on our way. It wasn't indifference, my mother told Aunty Madge, he literally didn't see the people staring. He didn't see the queue either and he ushered us all onto the top deck where we spread out across the two front rows for uninterrupted views of London, the best way to see the city, my father said. Jangling the money in his bag, the conductor came upstairs to take our fares.

'Hallo,' my father took out his wallet.

"Allo, mate,' replied the conductor, and then, looking round at all of us, 'Nice family you got there, they all yours?'

'One of them is my wife,' my father said stiffly. 'We are going to Victoria. How much is that?'

'You may be going to Victoria,' said the conductor, smiling, 'but this bus ain't.'

'I have been in England before,' my father said. 'I know that this is the bus for Victoria.'

'None of my business where you been. Look, if you're quick you can catch the one behind,' and he pointed at the back window.

Careful not to look at each other, we all trooped off the bus and onto the one behind. Having successfully negotiated that bus and then another, we arrived at Victoria Station, later than expected, but with my father's confidence restored. When we were comfortably settled on the train he looked around him, and, catching the eye of the passenger across the aisle, who was staring at us intrigued, my father informed him that we were off to spend the day at Sittingbourne and asked him if he knew the place.

'Charming spot,' the stranger said, 'but this train is not going there.'

Leaping to his feet, my father rushed to the door and, holding it open, exhorted us all to hurry or we would miss the train. A passing porter pointed us to the right train, which could be seen on the opposite platform all but steaming out of the station. Running fast now, we swept through the barrier and my father shouted to the guard as he put the whistle to his lips, 'Hold the train, we are not on board.'

The guard froze in disbelief, and we caught the train.

'You see,' said my father, 'it's not difficult in England when you know how.'

'All the same,' said my mother, 'I think we should take a taxi when we reach the other end.'

'Yes, I think that would be justified,' my father said, looking at his watch. 'Travelling on this train, which I did not expect, I calculate we are going to be two hours late.'

Unable to keep a straight face any longer, my mother said, laughing, 'It's easy when you know how.'

Dorinda and Johnny Everard were extremely polite when

we turned up two hours late for lunch. They had been missionaries in some of the remotest parts of the world and were probably used to even worse food than the meal they served to us, my mother said to Aunty Madge. But as Aunty Madge said, it couldn't have helped that the meal had become stone cold. My mother was forced to concede that that was not entirely their fault. My father said that he hoped their daughter Susan and I would become friends, a vain hope given that her most fervent pursuit was amassing Girl Guide badges. My father hoped too that Tunji and her brother Robert would be similarly well suited. I thought privately, the minute I saw him, that young Robert looked as if he had train-spotting blood in his veins, and, sure enough, that was his main hobby. Gerald would have eaten him for breakfast.

My father said he approved of the way English children followed hobbies and that we should acquire some too. Where could you buy them, my mother wanted to know.

'Go ahead, make fun of me,' my father said.

'I wouldn't dream of it,' my mother replied.

The Everards were the first of many of my father's friends whom we crisscrossed the country to visit. He seemed to have a soft spot for missionaries, I told Aunty Madge. To be fair, my mother said, they weren't all missionaries, but all the same she couldn't understand why he was dragging us all over the country in this way, because as far as she could see the visits were not proving a success. She had nothing to say to any of the wives and we generally disliked the children.

My father sailed for Nigeria after the Christmas holidays and my mother returned at the end of the following year. She took with her my two younger sisters, Yejide and Yinka, and left behind the elder one Aduke who joined me at school and, of course, my brother Tunji. It was then that we discovered why my father had been so assiduous in looking up his old friends and acquaintances. They were the ones who took us in for the holidays. I did not return to Aunty Betty and Uncle Theo in Croydon, nor did we stay with any other of Aunty Moira's relatives. My father wanted us to be in a more educative environment, he said. I must admit his decision caused me no grief; for one thing Gerald was no longer in Croydon, he had joined the Royal Air Force and, no doubt, would soon be flying proper aeroplanes. For another thing I had become, as Doreen had predicted, a proper little snob.

At Dove House I was their first African pupil but they were not my first English school so this time I was ahead. The worst they could do had already been done to me at Chilcott Manor. I had my defences prepared ready for any attack. I settled smoothly in, followed by my sister with scarcely a ripple. My mother wrote that Grandma had died, and I felt that because I had not kept her sufficiently alive in my heart she had not waited for me to come home. The break had been so complete and the transition so traumatic, it was impossible to believe that I would ever return. My life in Lagos seemed like a dream and Africa as remote as the moon. The camouflage markings became complete, it was as if I had been born again in England, there was nothing now to distinguish me from any other English schoolgirl: until the year I turned fifteen.

My father never remembered to let us know where we would be going until the very last moment, so it was not until the last week of term that we received a letter saying, much to our surprise, that all three of us would be spending the Easter vacation with Miss Faith Mitchell, a friend of Dorinda and Johnny Everard, whom we had first visited in Kent with my father more than two years before. Miss Mitchell had been a missionary too, apparently, and she lived near Bedford. We were not thrilled at the prospect of yet another missionary, but we were delighted not to be split up, because very few people were able or willing to accommodate three children for the holidays. We rejoiced too soon though, because two days later the unfortunate Miss Mitchell expired suddenly of a heart attack. 'And she hadn't even met us yet!' Aduke exclaimed bitterly as we removed the labels from our trunks.

On the very last day of term, having received another communication, Miss Bellamy was able to tell us that my brother would be staying with some people in Surrey, and my sister and I would be travelling to Birmingham to stay with friends there. We met briefly with my brother on the platform and waved him out of sight on the school train. It was a relief when our trunks were finally loaded with us onto the train; it had been too late to send the luggage in advance, and for the past few days they had been sitting in the hall corded up and, like us, awaiting news of their eventual destination.

We had given up all idea of anyone coming to meet us and I was looking around for a telephone when we spotted them walking hesitantly down the platform towards us: Mr and Mrs Braithwaite, the Baptist minister and his wife, in whose house we would be staying. As they came level, Mrs Braithwaite squinted discreetly down at our coat lapels, to see if we were wearing the name badges which had been issued to us at school. She was looking in vain because we absolutely never wore them, it was bad enough waiting around to be collected by complete strangers on a strange platform without compounding the indignity by wearing labels as if we were left luggage. This, of course, was not at all helpful to the unfortunate couples who came to claim us, but there was never any danger of them going away empty-handed; with years of experience behind us we could spot them instantly, even if they were in a crowd a hundred yards away.

'You must be the children we're looking for,' Mrs Braithwaite said, glancing around the deserted platform. 'You're not wearing your name tags I see.' And she laughed nervously.

My sister rewarded her with a look of withering contempt, as if to say, who else could we be? It was plain that she hated them on sight.

'Welcome to Birmingham,' Mr Braithwaite said kindly and unctuously, in tones with which we were now familiar, having stayed with clergymen of all denominations the length and breadth of the country. This couple looked, if anything, as bad as any we had hitherto encountered. However I rallied instantly, I was an even older hand at this than my sister; I had stayed in other people's houses for six whole years before she came on the scene, and I knew from hard won experience that, in this situation, the first impression was all important if our lives were to be at all bearable for the next few weeks.

Stepping smoothly in front of my sister, I said, 'Thank you, Mr Braithwaite, how very kind of you both to take us for the holidays. We are looking forward to our stay, and I'm sure we shall enjoy ourselves.'

'We shall certainly do our best to make you feel at home,' said Mrs Braithwaite, her fears allayed a little, smiling at us both. My sister declined to smile. She pulled her school hat low over her face and scowled all the way to the Braithwaites' house in the suburbs of Birmingham; she scowled throughout the conducted tour and despite surreptitious kicks on the ankle from me, refused categorically to be gracious. I admired everything. In the car I admired Mrs Braithwaite's hat, and through the windows I admired the view, although I privately thought Birmingham, flashing past, looked grim. On arrival I admired the house, the garden, our bedroom, and even the improving texts which graced the hospital-green walls in every room.

Mrs Braithwaite was delighted with me. 'I can see we shall get on splendidly together,' she said, ignoring my sister, who said she felt sick. The ride in the car had brought it on, Mrs Braithwaite supposed.

'No doubt,' I said.

'You are disgusting,' my sister said when finally we were alone, flopped out on the single beds in the privacy of our room. 'This house is horrible and so are the people, I hate them.'

I understood exactly how she felt. She was fed up with staying with all these different people. She was ten years old, and she still missed her mother.

Nevertheless I said, 'Whatever you may be feeling, it is best to make them like you, otherwise, as you must know by now, they will feel free to treat you badly, and there will be very little we can do about it.'

'I don't care whether they like me or not,' she said, 'they don't really want us here and I don't want to be here,' and she buried her face in her pillow. I felt very sorry for her.

My sister and I had developed strongly contrasting techniques for survival during the holidays. She refused to gloss over the fact that the families on whom we were farmed out did not want us, and we certainly did not want them. As far as she was concerned they would have to take her as they found her. She refused to charm or be charmed. She was prepared to take her chance and come out fighting. Hers was the narrow path of heroic resistance. But after my hideous experience when I first arrived in England of how cruel people could be, I knew where that path led. So now I was charm personified. Within a very few hours of meeting me the people with whom we stayed found themselves fired with a determination to make me (and of course my sister), so far from home, as happy and as comfortable as it was in their power to do. Knowing how much the odds were stacked against us, I left nothing to chance. When I tried I never failed.

In the evening we were introduced to Roly and Phil, Mr and Mrs Braithwaite's two sons. Roly, a sixteen-year-old Lego enthusiast, was still at school, and Phil had recently graduated as a teacher. He also taught in Sunday School, as did Carol, his fiancée, who joined us on this first evening for dinner. Carol was wearing ankle socks.

Over the fish pie in the green-painted, green-curtained dining room (green being Mrs Braithwaite's favourite colour, the colour, she said, of the fields of Elysium), Mrs Braithwaite explained to Aduke and me that although the highlight of our holidays would be the four days of the Easter weekend, which we would spend in church, Phil and Carol's engagement party was only one of the many exciting events we could look forward to while staying with them. She added that the party would be a genuine celebration from the heart, and not one of those occasions of artificial jollity induced by alcohol. Her family did not hold with alcohol. I agreed with her enthusiastically. Mrs Braithwaite said she hoped also that we liked music, as that was something that they enjoyed together as a family; they were particularly fond of Gilbert and Sullivan, and always stayed up to watch if a production were staged on the television. Aduke and I loved music, I declared.

'Well in that case we shall be able to include you in everything.' Mrs Braithwaite said delightedly, 'and do please, call me Mary.'

'Me too,' said Mr Braithwaite. 'You must call me Ernest.'

'If only I could take a book,' I said as we were preparing unenthusiastically for church the next Sunday. We were sitting in our room which was painted the same wan green as the rest of the house.

'You can take a book,' my sister said, throwing her hat in the air and catching it again.

'I wasn't being serious,' I said. 'Of course I can't.'

'Yes, you can, you can take the Bible,' she said gleefully, and, making a face, raced out of the door. I raced after her across the landing, and, leaping down the stairs, ran smack into Roly who looked alarmed at this indecorous behaviour on a Sunday, until I smiled at him. Roly smiled back, remembering no doubt that I had spent the whole of the evening before admiring his Lego reconstruction of the Pantheon in Rome.

'You are going to enjoy church, you know,' he said.

'Oh yeah!' my sister said.

'I'm sure we are,' I said.

We turned the corner into Graham Street and there, growing on the pavement before us, in the centre of Birmingham was a tropical garden in full flame. Twenty or thirty black ladies dressed to kill in saffron and scarlet and purple were clustered around the entrance of the Graham Street Baptist Church, like huge blooms of hibiscus and bougainvillaea, entirely eclipsing the rest of the congregation. They paused for a moment on the threshold, and then, moving magnificently, passed in a tight phalanx through the door.

'Who are they?' my sister and I asked, astonished.

Roly whispered to us as we took our seats inside that they were Jamaicans who had come to England to find work, and that, shamefully, they had not been welcome in some of the other churches in Birmingham. However his father was only too pleased to have his church filled every Sunday, and weekdays as well.

'There will be many more of them at the Easter service,' he said. 'They're a very devout lot of people.'

Nevertheless, in spite of the Jamaicans, the Graham Street Baptist Church looked dull even in comparison with the local parish church we attended each Sunday at school, and the prospect of spending the next two and a half hours within its undistinguished confines was not exactly enticing. There was nothing here to look at; no stained glass windows, no fluted arches or decorative screens, and no tombs or carvings. And with no doubt the usual fare of lugubrious hymns punctuated by parrot prayers and an interminable sermon; one hour was quite sufficient to worship God, I thought glumly.

Mr Braithwaite announced the hymn number, the organist struck up the first notes and we rose to our feet to sing. Before we reached the second verse, a large Jamaican lady dressed in heliotrope and orange madder, twirled out of her seat and leapt like a hare down the aisle with her arms outstretched to heaven. She was nimbly followed by another who passed by in a blur of shocking pink and peacock blue, another in swathes of lavender and lime, and another and another, until there was a line of ladies jumping up and down, glowing like a sunrise, singing and clapping, in praise of the Lord. Unable to contain ourselves, the rest of the congregation joined in, joyfully swinging it and winging it in time to the syncopated rhythms being belted out with such fervour by our Caribbean neighbours. Indeed on this occasion the sermon came as a welcome and necessary respite to catch our breath and gather ourselves for the final blast.

When Mr Braithwaite asked us afterwards if we had enjoyed ourselves, we were able to answer quite truthfully that we had. The worship of God, Mr Braithwaite said, was a joyful thing. Even so he must have been surprised at first when the West Indians started jumping around like that, I said.

'It was a shock initially,' Mr Braithwaite replied, 'but as you can see we get along very well together. I personally welcome their exuberance. Wait until you see them on Easter Sunday, that will be something.'

It looked as if I might have to revise my opinion of the Braithwaites.

On Easter Sunday when we turned the corner by the church, we were surprised yet again; the tropical garden had spread to both sides of the street and become a park. Today the West Indian ladies had outdone themselves, a rainbow would have appeared drab beside their shimmering silks and restless taffetas, and their raised voices were as vigorous and vibrant as the colours.

Standing in the midst of the commotion, surrounded by their friends and relations, the candidates for baptism were conspicuously quiet; tense with suppressed emotion, they wore studiedly beatific expressions and long flowing robes. On the outskirts of the crowd, curious bystanders looked on, magnetised, as if the circus had come to town.

In the packed church the atmosphere was volcanic with anticipation, as the organist, not to be outdone by the accompanying trumpets and tambourines, pulled out all the stops and led us into the first hymn like a man possessed. The voices of the congregation roared out to join him. We sang and clapped and stamped our feet until, exhausted, we sank into our seats for the sermon. The ladies fanned their necks just as they used to in Lagos cathedral. God was everywhere, Mr Braithwaite said, and the candidates certainly bore this out when they gave their personal testimony of how each of them had found him. God could catch you unawares, on the buses, in the post office, maybe even on the lavatory, my sister suggested from the side of her mouth.

I am afraid they didn't convince us, and God remained as unlikely to my sister and me on the night shift in Birmingham, as He did in the fields and woods around school, which was where the Reverend Mr Nixon of St Anne's was fond of telling us to look for Him. We knew that if God was anywhere He was up in the rafters of Lagos cathedral, held fast by Lagos society, which had exclusive rights over Him.

What could not be disputed though was that church in Birmingham was far and away the most fun.

Rising to our feet, we clapped and stamped again as one by

one the candidates in their long gowns, weighted at the hem for modesty, Roly said, were handed down into the baptismal pool to Mr Braithwaite who took them in his hands and ducked them backwards into the water, completely immersing them in the Name of the Father, the Son and the Holy Ghost, and then when their heads popped back up above the surface, he retrieved them deftly as if bobbing for apples in a barrel.

The service continued long into the afternoon and afterwards there was food and drink and gossip in the church hall. My palms stung and my voice was hoarse with singing, for the music and the clapping and the dancing had awoken fierce memories of the rhythms of home. Taking a plate of food, I crossed eagerly to join the rainbow circle.

'I liked the music,' I said, pushing in next to a lady in saffron and puce, and who was not unlike how I remembered Grandma. 'It sounded just like home. Jamaica must be exactly like Africa. Is it?' I finished brightly, looking round.

Complete silence engulfed the circle as everyone stared at me. The lady in saffron and puce did not reply, but finally a lady in electric green opposite said in disbelief, 'You from Africa?'

'Yes, Nigeria,' I replied.

'The West Indies is not like Africa at all,' she said, stretching her neck haughtily. 'It just like England in Jamaica.'

'Is that so,' I said, and, hurt and disappointed I turned away to join my sister.

For Phil and Carol's engagement party, the church hall was festive once again. Mrs Braithwaite had made sandwiches and sausage rolls and fruit cup. The hall was decorated with streamers and fairy lights, to put us in the mood for dancing, Roly said. He and I were watching some of the younger guests – Phil and Carol's friends from teacher training college and not one of them under twenty-five – 'dancing', slowly for the waltz and a little faster for the quickstep, though their movements were unconnected to the music which appeared incidental as if a tap had been left running. The older guests were not dancing at all, but sat stiffly in their chairs watching the dancing. Roly said he thought Carol looked pretty.

'Yes,' I said, although I thought that in her white dress she made Phil, who was steering her backwards round the floor, look as if he were carrying a big bunch of droopy daisies. Roly did not say I was pretty, he said I was the most sensible girl he had ever met, chiefly because I was the first girl who had been able to appreciate the finer points of his Lego. He had developed a crush on me and clung to my side all evening. My sister said it was my own fault for being such a hypocrite. I must say that when Mrs Braithwaite made Roly and me dance together I did think for a moment that perhaps my sister's system might work better in this situation than mine. She, who had been nothing but disagreeable since the day we had arrived, was being left to do exactly as she pleased, while I, who had ingratiated myself so effectively, was in imminent danger of being liked to death.

I had to admit that at the end of the evening Roly's Aunt Joan, who Roly said was rich and never went to church, and whom I had observed taking surreptitious nips from a flask in her bag, expressed my sentiments exactly when she suddenly shouted out that she could remember having had more fun at a funeral; mind you I had never been to an English funeral, and I couldn't help wondering if English funerals fell as far short of Nigerian standards as did this party. In my opinion Phil and Carol's engagement party would have benefited greatly from the presence of a few of the Jamaicans who had been in church on Easter Sunday.

In fact there was a simpler solution than inviting West Indians to an English party to make it go with a swing, as I discovered when Aunt Joan celebrated her son Robert's twenty-first birthday. She had willingly agreed to include my sister and me on the invitation to the Braithwaites, a testimony to my way of doing things, I said to my sister, but, shrugging her shoulders sceptically, she reminded me of Phil and Carol's party saying it was too early to tell.

Mrs Braithwaite was very proud of Roly that evening; straightening his tie as we were waiting for the taxis, she said she thought he looked very spruce in his evening dress. To be fair, it was pristine compared with his school blazer, which had more marks on it than a leopard has spots, and the jacket was managing to remain fastened across Roly's fine stomach in spite of the tremendous strain being placed on it by the Lego bulging out of the pockets. So it was not a complete untruth to nod my head in agreement with Mrs Braithwaite.

I ignored the sharp dig in my ribs from my sister; her gesture was misinterpreted by Mrs Braithwaite who kindly complimented us on our appearance too. She had personally chosen our new dresses, overriding our protests by saying that this being England she knew best what we should wear. Suffice it to say that we were laid as low by Mrs Braithwaite's fashion sense as the South American Indians were upon contact with the Spaniards. Aduke, whose looks were aquiline and severe, was in frills up to the neck, with puff sleeves and a bow, while my dress of tender apple green sagged loosely around me like a poster hanging from a wall, having no glue to keep it on, neither bosom nor hips.

The sound of the festivities could be heard long before we reached Aunt Joan's house. Mrs Braithwaite said she feared it was going to be a difficult evening, and Carol, who was sitting in front with the driver, said she feared so too. My sister said she thought the noise sounded promising. I kept silent. A magnificent marquee which Phil, who had been travelling in the car behind with Roly and Mr Braithwaite, said must have cost a pretty penny, had been erected on the lawn, and as we approached, the music from the band billowed out to meet us. Inside our eyes were dazzled by the light which spilled extravagantly down from half a dozen chandeliers and gilded the whirling couples on the dance floor.

My sister and I stared in astonishment, we had never seen English people in uninhibited enjoyment like this before, and very soon, having successfully shaken off Roly, we were lost in the crowd intoxicated by the scent of the flowers, and the fizz and bubble of the champagne. Aunt Joan, dashing past, asked if we were having a good time. Yes, we answered fervently. But at the same moment Mrs Braithwaite, who had come to stand beside us, shuddered.

'My sister has been drinking alcohol,' she said. 'It is quite unnecessary, one can enjoy oneself perfectly well without the use of artificial stimulants. It is a habit you especially should be careful not to acquire.'

'Oh?' I said.

'You people are particularly susceptible. I understand alcohol wreaks dreadful havoc in Africa.'

'I am sure you're right,' I said, and both of us turned to look at Aunt Joan who, on fire with diamonds, was scorching her way through a tango.

I did not agree with Mrs Braithwaite. Now that I had had two glasses of champagne and had been to two grown-up English parties, it was as clear as daylight to me that for a party to succeed in England, it was absolutely essential that there be some West Indians present, or, failing them, large amounts of alcohol, and maybe, I thought as I took another gulp of champagne, even both.

The Braithwaites were away for a week at a church conference which I managed to avoid only by insisting that my little sister could not possibly cope without me for all that time. Mrs Braithwaite took a great deal of persuading to leave me behind because, as she said, she was beginning to feel that I might have the makings of a future missionary in Africa.

Aduke and I were sent to stay with Aunt Joan and the visit turned out to be a revelation, just as her party had been. I suddenly saw clearly why Aunt Joan and her friends were different from the Braithwaites and all the other friends of my father's, with whom we had been staying over the past couple of years. They made no attempt to instruct or improve us; and nor did they behave as if it were necessary to be constantly vigilant for signs of degenerate pagan behaviour, as if at any moment we might revert, as one dear lady had put it.

'This week with Aunt Joan,' I said to my sister, as we lounged in garden chairs on the terrace and watched the daffodils dance in the spring sunshine while doing nothing whatsoever to improve the shining hour, 'has made me realise what it is that Daddy's friends, and the friends of his friends, have in common: the sight of our little faces impels them all to assume the missionary position.'

'And what's that?' she asked.

'An unhealthy interest in saving the heathen,' I replied.

'You see, I told you we shouldn't be nice to these people.' Which summed up the situation rather well, I thought.

The Easter holiday ended in disappointment. Mrs Braithwaite found on her return from the church conference that I did not after all have the makings of a missionary and I was dismayed at finding her, despite the welcome given to the West Indians, tarnished as it were. I was saddened too by the Jamaican ladies' reaction, after the first occasion I never dared approach them again, but the feeling of kinship persisted and was packed away with the rest of my belongings for the return to school. The aeroplane paint was flaking away the older I grew.

Chapter 10

'Your father's a nut,' Phoebe Vincent said sympathetically when I had finished describing the Braithwaites, 'like my mother.' Phoebe was my best friend in Dove House and she knew what she was talking about, her mother smoked a pipe and was knowledgeable about art. Miss Bellamy, our headmistress, who liked Phoebe, and me too it must be said, was always careful to explain on open days that her mother was part foreign. Phoebe always wished on those occasions that her mother would go and live in Nigeria.

Christabel Harris, the most beautiful girl in the school, the town and quite possibly, it was thought, the world, said that she and her closest friend Joanna Mildmay would be spending their next vacation in Germany and why didn't Phoebe and I come along too.

'How?' we said.

'Easy!' Christabel said. 'My mother will arrange it.'

As we were not permanently resident in Worcester, Phoebe and I did not qualify for a place on the German trip, which was an exchange of young people between our school town and its newly twinned sister, Hessich-Neustadt, about fifteen kilometres from Hannover. However, when Christabel told her mother we were keen to go, she saw to it that we were included in the party, for her mother, who had an extensive wardrobe of jewel-coloured duster coats and a big haughty nose, sat on the committee. In fact, as Christabel said, there wasn't a committee in Worcester that Mrs Harris did not sit on. Well primed by us, Mrs Harris was careful to stress the educational nature of the exchange when she proposed my going to Miss Bellamy, and Miss Bellamy followed her example when on my behalf she made her representation to my father. Thus he was persuaded and I, as Phoebe put it rather dramatically, was saved from the maw of the missionaries. More dramatic still though was Phoebe's sudden withdrawal from the excursion. Her mother telephoned Mrs Harris at the last minute to say that she could not allow her daughter to visit Germany, because she found that she was unable after all to forgive the Germans. Phoebe's grandmother it transpired was partly Jewish. Mrs Harris said there would be hell to pay if I withdrew too and frankly, although she quite understood, she felt that one should let bygones be bygones.

As luck would have it, for this vacation my father had arranged for Tunji, Aduke and me to stay not with missionaries, but with two friends of his who promised to be even more fun than Aunt Joan. Charles and Leonora Wilshire were both barristers and, having no children of their own, also happily had no preconceptions of how children ought to behave. It was with real regret that after one week, spent at their house in Hampstead, I left for Germany while they travelled down to their house in Wales, taking my brother and sister with them. In that one week, I bragged, quoting Charles, they had introduced us to the recondite pleasures of the Sir John Soane Museum in Lincoln's Inn and the Physic Garden in Chelsea; while we in turn initiated them into the arcane mysteries of the world of teenagers and rock and roll music.

'Oh yeah?' Christabel and Joanna, eyes fixed on the distant lights of the approaching Hook of Holland, were unimpressed. I gave up and directed my eyes also towards the horizon. There was precious little to see, I thought.

None of us in the party from Worcester had ever been abroad before. Nigeria didn't count, Christabel said, and I agreed as it was so long ago. The thing that struck us first was that their eggs and bacon were laughable, as Joanna said, expressing our collective disgust at breakfast on the train. They had no idea how to cook them at all.

Knowing no one else in the group, whose members apart from us three had all been culled from the two grammar schools in Worcester, I stuck fast to Christabel and Joanna and all three of us were squeezed into the same seat as our bus drew into the cobbled gingerbread square in the centre of Hessich-Neustadt. The Mayor, his wife, the whole of the Town Council and, it appeared, the entire population had turned out to meet us. The Mayor launched into his speech of welcome as soon as the first of us began leaving the bus, but when I appeared in the doorway, my foot poised on the top step ready to descend, he stopped. Silence fell. Everyone stared at me including the members of my own party who turned around to find out what on earth could be the cause of such consternation.

The good people of Hessich-Neustadt had clearly never seen an African before, or, if they had, they had forgotten, and as they gasped and stared and pointed, the African, panic-stricken, disappeared backwards into the bus again as swiftly as a rabbit down its hole.

'I am not leaving this bus,' I said.

'Oh God,' Christabel said, 'I bet nobody thought to tell them.'

'Tell them what?' asked Joanna.

'That Remi was from Nigeria.'

'I don't care,' I said, 'I am never leaving this bus.'

'I wish Mummy were here,' Christabel said, 'she would know what to do.'

'She was the one who filled in the form,' I said ungratefully.

Miss Parkes, one of the four teachers in charge of the party, came in and said, 'Remi, you will have to face the music some time, so you might as well get it over with straight away. It will be much better for you. Come on now, our hosts are waiting to welcome us outside. You don't want to disappoint them, do you?'

Eventually, flanked by Christabel and Joanna who held on to my arms to prevent me from bolting back into the bus a second time, I came and stood outside with the others, keeping my eyes steadfastly on the ground. And the Mayor resumed his speech.

When he had finished, our names were called out one by one and the families with whom we would be staying stepped forward to claim us. When I heard my name I closed my eyes and willed myself to vanish into thin air; instead my hand was gripped in a vice. I looked up and could not suppress a gasp now myself; the most enormous man I had ever seen in my life clicked his heels – the sound seemed to reverberate around the square – and bowed his head before me. His son Wolfgang, twelve years old and as tall as me, copying his father exactly, showed me the top of his silvery crewcut crown. Wasting no time Herr Schöfbeck, for that was the name of my host, bore me off with Wolfgang in close formation behind through the crowd, which parted cleanly like the waters of the Red Sea, to a black limousine, identical to all the ones in the war films, which was drawn up at the side of the square.

Within seconds I was ensconced inside. I put my head out of the window. 'Christabel, Joanna,' I cried in desperation. 'When will I see you?'

But before they could answer, Herr Schöfbeck had slammed the doors and we sped out of town. Dejected, I slumped back on the seat.

The German countryside flashed past until at last the car turned up a drive and came to a stop in front of a large house which I took to be a typical Swiss chalet. Herr Schöfbeck ushered me up the steps and in through the door to meet the reception committee waiting inside: his wife Frau Schöfbeck; his mother Oma, beside whom Aunty Betty would have been the sugar plum fairy; his younger son Reiner; and his nephew Otfried, easily as big as Gerald who would have been extremely scornful of his short leather trousers.

The reception committee to my surprise did not turn a hair when they saw me. '*Guten Tag,*' they said.

'How do you do,' I said.

But I must admit that when Otfried had finished shaking my hand I would happily have given it away, it throbbed so.

Why was it, I asked, that I was staying miles out of town and away from everybody else. Miss Parkes said that the organisers had tried to match us all as nearly as possible to our own families, and that since Mrs Harris had stressed that my father was a Lord Chief Justice, I had been assigned to the most prominent family in Hessich-Neustadt. The Schöfbecks owned the sugar factory which was responsible for the town's prosperity, Miss Parkes said, and I supposed that this was why when we visited the sugar factory I was treated like a freak with people hanging on my every breath and scrutinising my every move like visiting Royalty; but I was wrong, as I was soon to find out.

I spoke no German, it was not one of my subjects at school. My forte was French but, alas, when I had tried my speciality on the Schöfbecks on the first night they had looked as perplexed as if I had been speaking my native Yoruba, which actually I no longer could.

'*Du Schwarz*,' Oma said, stabbing fiercely at the dictionary lying open on her voluminous lap. The two of us were alone: Frau Schöfbeck was preparing supper, Herr Schöfbeck and Otfried had not yet returned home and there was no sign of Wolfgang and young Reiner.

I riffled through the pages of my own minuscule Collins German Gem until I found the word. Black, the dictionary said. Here we go, I thought, and stabbed at a word in my turn. 'Afrika,' I said.

Oma eyed me speculatively, and I was suddenly reminded of the images of those northern witches which had so terrified me in those first nights at school in England. Oma could have crunched me up in a moment and not even noticed.

'*Schön*,' she said loudly, jabbing her finger at her book, making me jump.

Hurriedly I turned the pages of mine. Beautiful, I read. I wasn't expecting that. 'Thank you. *Danke*,' I said, pointing.

Herr Schöfbeck and Otfried came striding in and I leapt up to shake their hands, not wishing to make the same mistake as at breakfast. Eager to make a good impression, I had been first up after Frau Schöfbeck, not even the birds were up before Frau Schöfbeck, and I was so busy attacking what was to me a very novel breakfast of sausage and cheese that I did not notice anyone else come into the room. When I eventually looked up, there waiting in line silently observing me were Herr Schöfbeck, Otfried, Wolfgang and little Reiner, all of them unable to sit down until they had shaken my hand. I hated to think what would have happened if I had not looked up, so now I was on the alert. In between pointing out words in the dictionary we smiled and nodded at each other until our jaws ached and Frau Schöfbeck called us in to dinner.

Frau Schöfbeck was not quite as large as Oma but she clearly felt that anything less was not proper in a woman, because as she piled my plate high with potatoes and gravy she said, via Otfried, that although I was a beautiful girl I was too thin. She wanted me to grow big, big, Otfried said, demonstrating with his hands the shape Frau Schöfbeck thought suitable, approximately four times my present size.

'Ja, Ja,' Herr Schöfbeck said, nodding vigorously and pointing out the word 'slender' in the dictionary, which he had placed between us on the dining table.

Our timetable was arranged so that there were official outings and entertainments on alternate days, leaving us free on the others to participate in whatever activities our individual families had laid on for us.

My first free day was spent learning to ride a bicycle, because, as Otfried had pointed out to me, this was the only means of going into town. Frau Schöfbeck started me off in the morning and pretty soon I was careering around the garden on my own, scattering the geese and chickens, greatly encouraged by the yells of young Reiner and Oma, who was hanging out the washing.

Oma's main function apparently was to hang the clothes out on the line, which she did from morning till night, trudging backwards and forwards from the house with a huge basket on her hip. The clothes she wore never varied, she came downstairs each morning in a long black dress and a grey knitted shawl pinned across her breast. The shawl was identical in colour and texture to her hair which was plaited into two circular earphones over her ears. Oma was like the old gypsy woman in the poem, Meg Merrilies – elemental. Her brothers could have been the craggy hills, and her sisters the tall pine trees, because when she saw me heading uncontrollably on the bicycle towards a wall or a ditch, she calmly spread out her arms and stepped in front of me and I rode into her just as if she were a hedge or a grass verge. By the evening, although I still had problems stopping, Otfried declared himself satisfied that I could safely accompany him into town by bicycle provided that there was no other traffic on the road and I did not have to turn any corners.

Herr Schöfbeck, who along with everyone else had been watching my victory lap around the perimeter of the garden, was so tickled by this remark he struck me a friendly blow across the shoulders which would have put a less athletic girl than myself in hospital.

However I was unable to put my newly acquired skills into practice immediately because the next day was an official one, and according to the programme the English party was to spend the entire day at the school in Hessich-Neustadt.

Rumour had it that the school was coeducational. The schools in Worcester were single sex and strictly segregated, the opposite sex was considered a different species and treated as such. At Dove House the mistresses continually impressed on us the fact that *boys*, a word none of them could utter without a shudder, were more dangerous than the Vikings.

In response to Freddie Potter's question from the back of the bus, Mr Nicholls, who was sitting in front with Miss Parkes, confirmed that the school in Hessich-Neustadt was indeed, like all the schools in Germany, coeducational, and the mere thought of meeting so many eligible boys and girls made our hearts flutter violently against our sides on the quarter of a mile drive down the road.

At lunch Freddie Potter spoke for the boys when he said that the German girls were lookers all right, but he had to agree with Peter Thomson that not one of them could hold a candle to our own acknowledged beauty. Christabel Harris was hard to beat; her figure was petite, when she smiled her dimples showed and her dark blonde hair turned up naturally at the ends. The German boys weren't bad looking either, the girls thought, they had wonderful legs, but Freddie Potter argued that that was only because they were brown on account of wearing those damn silly shorts.

Christabel said that there had been nothing ridiculous about Hans Kuhlemann in his *Lederhosen* when he had stood up to welcome us this morning, and in this she spoke for the girls. Christabel, representing Dove House, was the last to speak in the afternoon and after a few nicely chosen words in response to Hans Kuhlemann, she went on to explain what life was like in our school and it was not clear from the bemused expressions on the faces of her listeners whether she had indeed succeeded in conveying something of the esoteric flavour of an English girls' boarding school or whether they had simply not understood. She sat down to tremendous applause, and Joanna Mildmay and I clapped loudest, enjoying the reflected glory.

'Thank you, that was very good,' the German teacher said. 'And now we would like to hear about Africa.'

We looked up in surprise, who was going to tell them about Africa? Joanna Mildmay nudged me in the ribs. 'He means you,' she said.

'Why me?' I said. 'I don't know anything about Africa. Can't they see I'm from England like everyone else?'

'Come, Remi,' said Miss Parkes, 'don't be shy, I'm sure you must have something interesting to tell us about your native land.'

'Actually I don't,' I said.

'For goodness' sake,' whispered Freddie Potter, 'you can think of something, tell them anything, we'll be here all day otherwise.'

Well I certainly wasn't going to tell them anything about Lagos and my family, I thought, as I walked up to the front of the classroom, and it would be too risky to improvise on any film plots.

'My father is a chief,' I began, exactly as I used to years ago at Chilcott Manor, 'a chief of the Masai tribe. The Masai are cattle herders and great warriors.' I described as faithfully as I could remember the article I had read in the *National Geographic Magazine* about these noble people who lived in East Africa somewhere. I'd found the story fascinating and so did my audience, my ovation was nearly as long as Christabel's.

'I almost believed you myself,' she said when I sat down again beside her. Miss Parkes said she thought Dove House had reason to be proud of its pupils.

We visited the famous city of Hamelin and, as Miss Parkes said, played the Pied Piper ourselves, helping to rid the citizens of the present plague of chocolate and marzipan rats by consuming so many of them. After inspecting the murals depicting the famous legend in the town hall, poetically called the Ratcatcher's House, the Mayor, who had stared at me throughout, rushed home to fetch his wife and asked me if I would have my photograph taken with them. I was the first African, they said, to have visited the place.

'No,' I said.

But Miss Parkes insisted that I be a good sport and comply with his request. Relations between Miss Parkes and myself were rapidly deteriorating, and when she suggested I wave to the hordes of children who had followed us to the banks of the River Weser when all I wanted to do was to push them in, they were strained to breaking point.

Miss Parkes and I stopped speaking altogether when, again as the first African, I was asked to plant a tree and I refused. I told Miss Parkes that I felt I was being treated like a freak. Yes, she said, but I was being treated very nicely nonetheless. I was unusually silent on the bus going back to Hessich-Neustadt.

'What's the matter?' Christabel asked. 'Cat got your tongue?'

'No,' I said, 'I was thinking.'

'She can't be well,' Christabel said to Joanna, laying her hand on my forehead. 'What were you thinking?'

I'd been thinking in fact that our social life was due to begin in earnest. The Gymnasium had broken up today, and the flower of the youth of Hessich-Neustadt would be sunning itself beside the Olympic proportions of the municipal swimming pool, and we, the English party, would be there too, before, as Freddie Potter put it, going on to dance through the night, ho ho ho! I was now looking forward to these activities with a certain amount of dread, because I very much feared that the youth might treat me in the same way as their elders, like a freak.

'I was thinking,' I said to Christabel, 'that I hope no one will ask me to do anything fancy in the swimming pool tomorrow on account of my being the first African to have swum in it.'

'I hope not too,' Joanna said promptly, 'because if they do, given how well you swim, you will also be the first African to have drowned in it.'

It was obvious from the start that first choice for all the boys was Christabel Harris. Added to her other advantages, her mother had had the good sense to buy her a ruched turquoise one-piece which emphasised her bust and tied in a bow at the back. Joanna and I sat on either side of her, silently cursing our mothers in our school regulation navy blue, fine for swimming sports but with zero après-swim appeal. Christabel had eyes for no one but Hans Kuhlemann, first choice for all the girls.

Life wasn't fair, but it wasn't bad either, as Freddie Potter said. I agreed, I was not so far being treated as a freak. Nevertheless by the end of the afternoon everyone in the English party was pretty well fixed up. I pointed this out to Joanna as we strolled in our identical bathing suits to the edge of the pool for a last dip, prior to her gracefully diving in and me jumping in holding my nose. She said she was sure that some of the boys did fancy me but my being so conspicuous made them shy to approach me. That was one way of looking at it, and I decided to look at it that way for the time being and wait and see what befell in the evening.

Otfried kindly accompanied me back from the swimming pool as he had accompanied me there, with a stabilising hand placed firmly on the back of my bicycle seat, and this time the journey was completed without a single excursion into the ditch which, as he said, was a distinct improvement.

When we arrived the lamps were already lit, and the house

built all of wood shone like a jewel, handsomely repaying the long hours of Frau Schöfbeck's patient polishing. Even as we entered she was removing an invisible speck of dust from the newel at the foot of the stairs. Like a mirror it faithfully reflected her large pale face roped securely by her plaits. She greeted us warmly and stepped aside to let us pass up the stairs and then with her duster quickly removed the finger marks we left behind.

When I reappeared for supper in my best dress, ready for the dancing afterwards, I was showered with compliments.

'Wonderful. Beautiful,' Oma shouted, walking round me with the dictionary dangling from her hands.

Frau Schöfbeck circled my waist with her hands and shook her head. Herr Schöfbeck, Otfried, Wolfgang and little Reiner all joined in the praise. They behaved as if I were a raving beauty. I was flattered but I thought they were mad, aberrant. My nickname at school, admittedly amongst my enemies, was the Gorilla.

In honour of my best dress Otfried and I rode into town in the limousine with Herr Schöfbeck, who dropped us at the entrance to the Beer Garden before roaring off to an appointment of his own.

'Over here,' Freddie Potter shouted, and with a wave to Otfried I joined my friends at their table under the trees which were festooned with lights. Up on the stage the band was playing a waltz, stringing the notes like beads on the soft night air.

'Like your dress,' Joanna and Christabel said as I sat down. Looking around I saw that everyone was here from the swimming pool and many more whom I did not recognise. A boy sitting at the next table introduced himself as Franz and asked me to dance. I exchanged a knowing smile with Joanna and walked ahead of him towards the dance floor. The instant we reached it, however, I realised too late that I should not have accepted the invitation. His friends began to clap and cheer, they were obviously expecting to have some sport. The other couples, realising this, quickly dropped out so that Franz and I were the only two left on the dance floor. The tempo quickened and Franz began to roll his eyes and cut the most amazing capers. I refused to be drawn, however, and, growing redder and redder in the face, he was forced to give the 'exhibition' on his own. When the music stopped I walked back to my seat looking neither to the right nor the left, and this time Joanna and I avoided each other's glance.

Joanna had been wrong this afternoon at the swimming pool, the boys had not merely been shy after all. Nobody else asked me to dance except Otfried, who asked me to dance again and again. The stars, he said, were no brighter than my eyes, but I knew that was because the stars did not have tears in them; confirming what I had also earlier suspected, that he was mad. Or maybe it was just that he was old; he was, as Christabel pointed out, in this summer of our sixteenth birthday, well on the wrong side of twenty-one.

Herr Schöfbeck announced, just as my father would have done, that he was taking me out for the day. Otfried protested, he had planned to take me bicycling, but his uncle would brook no argument, he wanted to show me the German countryside which, he said, was superb, and afterwards we would visit his brother who lived on a farm.

I had imagined that we would be travelling in the limousine, but I was mistaken, waiting outside was a large and powerful motorbike. Herr Schöfbeck strapped a huge pair of goggles to my head, invited me to get up behind him and instructed me to hold onto him tightly around the waist in order that I should not fall off. I did my best but it was like trying to grip a giant redwood around the waist, and I saw precious little of the German countryside because, on account of Herr Schöfbeck's girth, I was forced to sit with my face either pressed into his back or crooked up horribly towards the sky. At each of the level crossings, which were legion, the other road users descended from their cars and came to stand and stare at me, impaled on Herr Schöfbeck's back like a butterfly under glass, until the train had passed and they all climbed into their vehicles again. Herr Schöfbeck accelerated swiftly away leaving them behind, until they caught up once more at the next one. It was a great relief to spend a few hours recuperating at the farm before the return journey when the road users behaved in precisely the same way, so that I went to bed that night suffering from acute paranoia.

I was awoken by Herr Schöfbeck creeping in through the french window in my room, which opened onto the same balcony as his own. Amazed, I sat bolt upright with my plaits, equally surprised, standing straight up on my head. Herr Schöfbeck put his finger to his lips for silence and sat down on the end of my bed. Suddenly aware of my nakedness, I hastily dragged the bedquilt up to my chin thereby exposing my legs and feet.

'I have some chocolate for you,' Herr Schöfbeck said, playfully tickling my feet.

I quickly retracted them but he determinedly pursued my toes under the covers with one hand while popping squares of thin bitter chocolate into my open astonished mouth with the other. I could not at first imagine what had come over Herr Schöfbeck, but when he began to point out words like lithe and sinuous in the dictionary, I realised that Otfried was not alone – Herr Schöfbeck had taken a definite fancy to me too. I confided as much to Christabel and Joanna.

'What kind of chocolate is it?' Joanna wanted to know.

'I don't know and I don't like it,' I said.

'Which, the chocolate or Herr Schöfbeck?' Giggling, Christabel sucked on her straw as if it were a cigarette.

'Both,' I said shortly, blowing down mine and creating frothy bubbles in the bottom of my glass.

'You obviously appeal to sophisticated tastes,' Christabel said.

'Why, because my only two admirers are in their dotage?'

'But Otfried is handsome, you have to admit.' Joanna put her glass down and, holding the edge of the table, rocked her chair precariously onto its back legs.

'You must pretend to be asleep,' Christabel advised, looking wise.

'Fancy a dip?' Joanna asked, bored.

'No,' I said and watched glumly as the two of them walked towards the edge of the pool. I decided to take Christabel's advice.

I had reason to be grateful to the Schöfbecks, though, because on unofficial days when it came to pairing or teaming up, the boys in the English party and the young men of Hessich-Neustadt ignored me altogether, and on official days I was singled out at every opportunity as something outlandish and extraordinary. You would have imagined, judging from the reaction I received here, that the camouflage paint had peeled away completely: the Germans apparently did not see in me an ordinary English schoolgirl like any other. But then, I thought, what did they know?

– Chapter 11 –

'So how was it, how was Germany?' Phoebe asked.

'It was weird,' I said, 'I was treated like some kind of freak and they kept asking me about Africa.'

'Surely they must have seen that you're no longer African. The thing that strikes one immediately about you, my mother says, is how very English you are.'

'Not any more apparently. The Germans didn't seem to think so.'

'I imagine it's because they don't speak English, if they did they'd soon realise.'

'Maybe.'

'What's far more important, however, is how did you go down with the boys?'

I rolled my eyes heavenwards and shook my head.

'They thought you were ugly.'

'Thank you very much! But . . . yes now you mention it.'

'Not one single chap fancied you?'

'No. Well, there was the old man I was staying with, who gave me chocolate, and his nephew; but he was twenty-five if a day.'

'What kind of chocolate?'

'Phoebe!'

'I'm sorry. Thank goodness I didn't go after all.'

We couldn't know for sure of course, but it was fair to say that in her own way Phoebe was as far removed from the commonly held ideal of beauty at Dove House as I was. Gloomily, feet up on our desks in the deserted sixth form class room, we contemplated the coming year.

Traditionally, because there were no exams at the end of it, the first year in the sixth form was devoted to the serious pursuit of boys, and all the criteria previously thought desirable changed overnight. Being clever and good at games for example were now positively undesirable. Success was measured entirely according to how popular you were with the opposite sex, and to be popular with them, as everybody knew, you had to have looks, and not only that, your looks had to conform to a very precise standard: you had to be as near as damn it the spitting image of Sandra Dee or Debbie Reynolds; petite, blonde and curvy and in no wise capable of defending goal in hockey or throwing a cricket ball for any length. Christabel Harris could have been mistaken for either. For Phoebe and myself, on the other hand, it would have been futile even to aspire. As had been frequently pointed out, Phoebe's hair was exactly the colour of school gravy, and the only feature I had in common with Debbie Reynolds or Sandra Dee was eyebrows. Germany had confirmed our worst fears that the same standards obtained in the outside world as in Worcester and at Dove House.

Mr Lawson our English master was no exception.

'What a treasure trove of beauty lies before me,' he said, looking into Christabel's eyes. 'I refer of course to these,' and he lowered his gaze to the books spread out on the table in front of him. 'Byron, Keats, Shelley, Jane Austen and the Brontes!' All six of us in the Advanced Level English set beamed at him eagerly like pointers poised to retrieve. 'Chaucer,' he continued, 'oh how I envy you! And the greatest of them all, William Shakespeare.'

The work would not be easy, Mr Lawson said, the standard required at Advanced Level was virtually the same as in the first year at university. Then he said, waggling his hand in my direction, 'We will have to make allowances for Remi, she will find it particularly difficult as she does not have the same cultural heritage.'

I was quite literally dumbfounded; I stared at Mr Lawson, we all did. Last year in my Ordinary Level exams I had achieved the highest possible grades, as he well knew, and I was intending to read English at university. It was as if he had pressed a button and slid an invisible panel between my friends and me. We could see each other as before, but I had the impression that now if we tried to touch we would feel the glass there dividing us.

'The set play this year,' Mr Lawson continued, 'is *Othello*.'

'He's obviously gaga,' Phoebe said later.

'I'm not so sure,' I said.

Despite maximum exposure on the debating team and coveted roles as serving wenches in the Carlton College Christmas play, neither Phoebe nor I acquired any admirers. We failed to score in the La Ronde coffee bar on our Saturday visits to town, and similarly on our Sunday afternoon walks, where boys from the surrounding schools, taking their own walks, were thicker than thistles on the route. At Easter we retired from the lists, having received no post on Valentine's day. Literature, we decided, was a preferable pursuit. Our application brought its own rewards when Janet Lawrence, who had huge baby blue eyes but also, as Christabel unkindly remarked, trouble spelling her name, approached us to help her pen a letter to her beloved. She very much admired, she said, the extracts from our essays which Mr Lawson read out in class. Flattered, we agreed. The letter achieved such spectacular results that word soon spread and we were writing love letters for the whole of the sixth form, including Christabel Harris. We took particular care with the letters to her many admirers because her reputation as the most desirable girl in town reflected well on all of us at Dove House. In this way, as Phoebe said, she and I were able to communicate, at least vicariously, with the objects of our desire.

In class too our literary efforts were crowned with success. Mr Lawson said it was remarkable, quite remarkable, I was to be congratulated on coming first in the class exams. But he was quite unable to disguise the fact that he was most put out.

'The old boy's really furious with you for coming top,' Phoebe said in some surprise.

'Not as furious as he is with you for coming second,' I replied.

'Yes but why?' she said. 'I can't work it out.'

'I imagine it's for the same reason that Miss Desmond changed the rules and awarded the Victor Ludorum Cup on sports day to Jane Whittaker, "who had tried hardest throughout the year," instead of to me, who actually won.' Playing the game, not winning, was the thing, Miss Desmond said.

'What is the reason?'

I looked across at Mr Lawson as he bent attentively over Christabel's desk, 'Don't you see, Mr Lawson is behaving like Desdemona's father, who could not understand how or why she had been induced to fall in love with a black man.'

'You mean he thinks there's something fishy going on?' Phoebe grinned. 'Come to think of it, so do I.'

'I'm being serious, remember my cultural disadvantages! As the old boy loves to point out, there's no written culture in my country. I'm sure he thinks I'm using some kind of voodoo to woo the language to me in the same way Brabantio accused Othello of using spells on Desdemona.'

'I get it!' Phoebe said, and triumphantly quoted Brabantio's lines. 'For nature so preposterously to err, Being not deficient, blind or lame of sense, Sans witchcraft could not. That's what Mr Lawson reckons.'

'I reckon,' I agreed, laughing.

'What was that, what did you say?' Mr Lawson spun round. 'Speak up.'

'We were discussing why it was that in Nigeria we did not manage to invent the wheel, Mr Lawson,' I said.

'You realise what all this means,' I said to Phoebe. We were sitting once again in the deserted sixth form class room, only now the windows were wide open and the candles in bloom on the horsechestnut trees. Our classmates were busy preparing for the Dove House School Dance, which, had it been possible, we would have avoided; alas, attendance was obligatory and we were postponing our preparations for as long as possible. 'It means that because of my public school education and upbringing, I have grown up thinking of myself as an Englishwoman, one of you, Desdemona, but now that I'm becoming an adult I suddenly discover that I am in fact Othello.'

'What on earth do you mean?'

'Othello was destroyed,' I declared, 'because his marrying Desdemona was seen as an attempt to become a Venetian, and the Venetians could not tolerate this in a black man. It has become increasingly obvious to me that if I do the same thing by trying to become one of you, I am likely to receive the same treatment. All this time I've been living in a fool's paradise and now I don't know who I am. It's a tragedy.'

'It doesn't have to be, at least now you know who you're not, you can begin to discover who you are,' Phoebe said unsentimentally. 'Climb down from your metaphor for a minute and think what we can do to improve our appearance for the ball. Here,' she said, holding out her long mud-coloured plaits for me to look at, 'you have a real tragedy.'

'Auburn highlights,' I said, examining them, 'that's what you need.'

Auburn highlights notwithstanding, we were midway through the Supper Dance and Phoebe and I had yet to be invited on to the dance floor. The Assembly Hall had been transformed, balloons and silver streamers fluttered from the ceiling, all the doors and windows were open and the air was filled with summer scents and the unaccustomed sound of deep voices. At least our colours did not clash, Phoebe said as the two of us sat side by side against the wall engaged apparently in animated conversation. That was something to be thankful for, I agreed, given that we were likely to pass the entire evening side by side.

Phoebe was wearing maroon velvet adapted by her mother, who, alas, was not entirely *au courant* with present-day fashions. She had done her best, but, as Phoebe said, what could you expect? Her mother had shingled hair and wore men's suits. It was a very individual look, I said to comfort her.

My taffeta dress was green; chosen for me by Mrs Braithwaite the year before, it still drooped on me. It had a sweetheart neckline and little cap sleeves and lent its colour to my skin, giving me the look of a tree tainted with mildew. Christabel Harris's dress matched the colour of her eyes, a hazy hyacinth blue, and as she drifted by in the arms of the captain of the College rugby team we could not help wondering how it would be if he knew who had really written those letters.

Supper came and went. We must be setting some kind of a record, Phoebe said as we sat again on our seats by the wall. But even as she spoke the words, Miss Bellamy appeared in front of us. Here were two young men who wanted to dance, she said. They did not look as if they wanted to dance at all. Miss Bellamy prodded them. May I have this dance? they said. Yes, we said. I didn't catch his name; he didn't have spots but he did wear glasses.

'My subjects are physics, maths and chemistry,' he said.

'English, French and history,' I replied.

We circled round the floor in silence, dancing was not one of his subjects either. A girl in hyacinth blue wafted by.

'I say isn't that . . .'

'Christabel Harris,' I said.

'She's very attractive,' he breathed.

I agreed. He peered at me then, a long look through his perfectly round National Health spectacles in their piggy-pink frames. 'I say,' he said, 'are you considered attractive in your own country?'

Intent as ever on defending the honour of Africa, and in all truthfulness I replied, 'No actually,' but I prayed that his life might be blighted.

My mother said, when I told her, that she was sorry to disappoint me, but far from his life being blighted, he was precisely the kind of young man destined for a brilliant diplomatic career in some Commonwealth country.

'Let us see the dress,' my father said. 'Aiyee!' he cried, when I appeared in it, 'who will we find to marry her?' My mother said only that there must be something seriously wrong with Mrs Braithwaite. She was very fond of green, I said.

Our parents were back (not before time, my sister Aduke

174

said) and installed in the house in Primrose Hill which my father had bought. It was time, he said, for the two youngest ones, Yejide and Yinka, to be put into school in England. My mother would be staying for a while, because it would be ruinously expensive, my father said, to have to pay for five children to be looked after during the holidays.

It was also true that Tunji, Aduke and I had exhausted the entire gamut of his friends and contacts: we had spent the previous three vacations at two establishments euphemistically known as children's holiday hotels, which catered specifically for children whose parents were abroad, in the main foreign children like ourselves, few of whom had been born west of Damascus. Major Shelley, recently retired from his tea plantation in Malaya, lined us up every morning to give us our tasks and also to put us on our honour to refrain from certain things: not to eat the strawberries, not to trample on the lawn and not to play ball near the drawing room windows. He invariably prefaced his requests by saying that he was aware that there was no concept of honour in the cultures we came from, but we ought to have grasped it by now having been in England for some considerable time. It was a fact that every day the drawing room reverberated to the sound of shattered glass, and by the end of the holidays, not only were our digestive systems severely impaired by a huge daily ingestion of strawberries, but also the ancient lawn, rolled for two hundred years, looked as if it had once again been put to the plough.

At Wickham House Miss Branston's obsession was Flamenco dancing, which she informed us she had taught in Argentina. Wasn't that coals to Newcastle? Aduke had wanted to know. It was in Argentina, Miss Branston said, ignoring her, and smiling fondly at her partner, that she had had the good fortune to meet Miss Beale. We spent the greater part of our time either touring the country in pursuit of visiting Flamenco troupes or thundering out our *Zapateado* on the boards Miss Branston laid down on the floor in the music room. It was fortunate that our nearest neighbour was the remand home for juvenile delinquents, who were in no position to complain. Just like us, my brother said. Parading in my green dress in front of my parents, I thought guiltily of Naomi, still there, whose mother sent her exquisitely embroidered dresses perfect for a six-year-old but much too small for her daughter at seventeen. It was a relief to know that my mother would be staying for a while, especially as for the next year I had nothing to 'do'.

I would not, in accordance with plan A, be going up to university this year to read English, but instead, in line with plan B, I would be going up the following year to read a subject of my father's choice. As far as Nigerians were concerned, there were only two subjects, medicine and law. Given the conspicuous absence of any science subjects among my qualifications, my father's choice was somewhat limited. I pointed this out to him. He was not amused. I could not blame him; at this rate if each of us added an extra year to our education it was likely to cost him more than the gross national product of, well, Upper Volta for example.

I had failed to gain a place at the college of my choice at London University because at the end of my interview I had been asked to read aloud a paragraph about a factory. Afterwards the professor, one of the four men sitting in front of me and with whom I'd been getting on like a forest fire, wondered if I could enlighten them as to the meaning of three simple little words, with which he was certain, he said, I would have no difficulty. The words were input, throughput and output. I enlightened him, feeling somewhat puzzled, factories until now having had no place in our discussions. The professor said that they asked this little test of all those students whose mother tongue was not English. I was taken aback, as I had been when Mr Lawson had first pointed out my cultural disadvantages.

In order to qualify for an interview I had had to write an essay, they knew my exam results, and furthermore they had been talking to me for nearly three-quarters of an hour. I lost my temper and my place. I had been foolish, my father said and, he said, to use a well-known English phrase, with which he was sure I would have no difficulty, I had thrown the baby

out with the bathwater. What was important, my father said, was that I knew that my grasp of the English language was equal to that of anyone born to it; whether or not those English professors acknowledged that fact did not alter it. I should remember this in future. I must have discovered by now, my father said, that Europeans believed many things about Africans that bore no relation to the truth. Did I know any Africans who conformed to their stereotypes? my father demanded.

I pointed out that I had not met many Africans recently and that it was difficult to maintain your confidence when you were the only African around.

Nonsense, my father said, I had no excuse, I was immensely privileged. He would have sympathised with my point of view, he said, had I been growing up in the Caribbean or America where the majority of black people faced almost insuperable odds. I was in England to obtain my qualifications and not to worry about what English people thought of me. Put like that, what could I say? Yes, I said.

Now, my father said, we should do something nice together. Must we? I protested. Yes, he said, we would go to the cinema. It was my own fault: with my sister and brother, I had accused him of having no idea of life as it was really lived in England and in order to rectify this, in addition to riding around on the tops of buses, he had taken up bingo and the cinema. He was now addicted to both.

We set off for the cinema and were stared at as usual; black people were a more common sight than they used to be but they were not by any means taken for granted. I was now so used to the stares I was able to behave as if I were oblivious to them. My father actually *was* oblivious to them and this made people stare even more. I had forgotten what it was like to be out in the street with him, that feeling that he might do something unusual at any moment. But he merely greeted people who took his fancy and introduced me to bingo friends we met along the way.

Did she think it was a good film, he asked the cashier as he bought the tickets, and did she think he would enjoy it? She

looked at him consideringly. 'I don't think I could speak for you, dear,' she said.

'Why not?' my father said.

'I think we should go in now,' I said, and hurried us in.

My father told the usherette that she must be sure to give him a good seat.

'You can have any seat you like,' she said.

'Thank you,' said my father and after much consideration we sat down. The villain crept up behind the hero with a gun.

'Watch out, he has a gun!' my father warned the hero and the cinema.

When the hero spun around my father thought this was due to him.

'I told you,' he cried.

The villain grabbed the heroine and held her with the gun in her back. My father turned to his neighbour. 'The man is a coward, not so?'

He continued his running commentary through the first minutes of the film, and then just as the people in the surrounding seats were contemplating climbing over them and murdering him, he fell asleep. I did not wake him until the very last moments and only then because he had begun lightly to snore.

'The picture is nearly ended,' I said, shaking him.

'I was not asleep,' my father said. 'He shot him, not so?'

'Not yet, any minute now,' his neighbour on the other side replied.

On the screen the villain crumpled to the ground.

'Aha! You see,' my father said, 'I was right.'

As we walked home my father said that it was imperative that this year while I waited to go to university should not be wasted. Paris would be a good place not to waste it, I replied, I could perfect my French. Paris would be a good place, my father agreed, but London would be better. I should take some law exams, he said.

Aunty Madge came to visit and a strange man appeared on the door step. My mother showed him into the drawing room.

'Who is he?' Aunty Madge asked her when she came back into the breakfast room where we were sitting.

'I have no idea,' my mother said. 'I thought he was a salesman when I opened the door. He must have some business with Simon. Remi, go and entertain him, Aunty Madge and I will follow you in when I've prepared the drinks.'

'What's his name?'

'He told me but I don't remember.'

Perched on the edge of the red velvet sofa, which my father had bought by the yard from the local furniture shop, and nursing a large gin and tonic, Mr Simms told us how he had met my father in a book shop in Piccadilly when they had both picked up a novel by William Golding and, finding that they also had Africa in common, Mr Simms having spent many happy years in Tanganyika, my father had kindly invited him to supper. We had of course been expecting him, my mother said, and my father would be home at any moment. Yes, Aunty Madge and I both nodded our heads when Mr Simms looked at us for confirmation. Reassured, he leant back on the sofa. My father brought him to the edge of it again however when he breezed into the room.

'And who are you?' he asked Mr Simms, shaking him warmly by the hand. Fortunately my mother had another gin and tonic ready and there was no problem about an extra person for supper either, because my mother, being African, always cooked as if an unexpected army might drop by.

Aunty Madge said my father hadn't changed, had he? He was as barmy as ever he was. My mother said she blamed the children for telling him he ought to get to know ordinary people. It was our fault too, she said, that she had now taken 'to no speak English' at the door whenever someone from the bingo queue turned up, as they frequently did, invited by my father; we had set her a bad example.

'That's easy,' Aunty Madge said, laughing, 'I'll know in future if I'm not welcome.'

'How's Gerald?' I asked Aunty Madge.

Gerald was married she said. I hadn't forgotten him, but I could not imagine what he might be like now, nor any of the others in the Stanley Terrace gang. I must say often on our rounds, staying with my father's friends, I had looked back nostalgically to my holidays in Thornton Heath, having learnt, contrary to what my first elocution mistress, Miss Clifford-Broughton had told me, that there were worse things in life than dropping your aitches. Now I could think of nothing to say, except to wish him happy.

'You'll be getting married yourself soon, I dare say,' Aunty Madge winked at my mother. 'You've turned her into a raving beauty.'

'Hardly,' I replied.

'Well a respectable near miss at any rate,' Aunty Madge conceded. 'It's amazing what your mother's achieved, I bet you're glad she's back.'

Aunty Madge was right, I was delighted with my mother. She had taken me out straight away to buy some clothes. Nothing in green, I said; I promise, she said. Soon it was as if she had never been away. Immediately my father left for Nigeria, my mother, well prepared this time, made the place her own. First she put the heating up. Whatever the temperature outside, it was permanently summer in our house, and then she filled the rooms with plants. Tiny pot plants, delighted at finding themselves back in the rain forest, grew into mighty trees in the twinkling of an eye.

'Blimey, if a parakeet flew out and landed on my 'ead, I wouldn't be surprised,' the gas man said when he came to read the meter.

I was delighted too not to be at university, to have a respite from being the only black girl in the class, the school, the faculty, maybe even the whole university for all I knew. But it was eerie, my youngest sister Yinka said, having only the three of us left in the house, Yejide having joined the other two at boarding school. We were not alone for long: Aunt Grace came to stay.

Aunt Grace had been married to Uncle Bode for several years now and she brought with her Uncle Bode's sister's child, Ebun, my cousin once removed, whom I had not seen since Sisi Bola's wedding, when both of us were five. Aunt

Grace removed her hat, which would have been perfectly at home in a game larder, and which prompted my sister Yinka to ask with interest what it was. I think she hoped it might have been for supper. While still in the hall, she asked if I had forgiven her for leaving me at school all those years ago. No, I said. Turning quickly to my mother, Aunt Grace declared that, if anything, the experience had been worse for her, the memory of my little face would haunt her to her grave, she said, shaking out her hair, which was as lustrous as ever.

Over her shoulder I exchanged a cynical glance with my cousin Ebun who, since Sisi Bola's wedding, had been like me at school in England. My mother suggested that we all come and sit in the room beside the kitchen; the estate agent called it the breakfast room, but it served as an inner courtyard in the centre of the house. My mother's big-leafed plants shut out the night and we sipped tea and nibbled chinchin while Aunt Grace relayed all the latest news from home. Her skin glistened in the tropic heat and you could smell the chillies frying on the stove.

Later in my room my cousin said, 'Everyone is here, you know.'

'Everyone?'

'Yes, all of us from Lagos, and that includes some gorgeous men. You remember all those boys we used to know, Akin Williams, Olu Thompson, Wole Grant: they've all grown up. The girls are here too of course, Ayo Smith, Dele Hopkins, Alaba Jones, all in London.'

'I remember the names,' I said. 'Where are they all?'

'Oh, around. You must meet them.'

I looked at Ebun resting daintily on one elbow in the middle of my bed; she looked very appealing, she could have auditioned for Bambi, and a horrible thought struck me.

'Do you think the men will find me attractive?' I asked.

'Of course they will,' she said, 'you're very good looking.'

And so I told her with actions the story of the school dance. She stared at me in horror, her eyes popping. 'Oh, Remi, that's terrible,' she said, but I could see as I finished indignantly that she was trying desperately not to laugh, and although she

clamped both hands across her mouth, snorts and giggles
escaped from her like bursts of steam until she blew up
altogether, bouncing up and down and drumming her feet
and fists on the bed. Well I supposed it was quite funny.
Wiping her eyes and still hiccoughing with laughter, she said,
'What did you say in reply?'

'I said, "No actually."'

Another paroxysm seized her. 'Why did you say that?' she
asked when she had recovered.

'I didn't want him to think African women were ugly,' I
said.

'Oh my God, I don't believe this,' she said and the tears
streamed down her face again. 'Show me,' she said. 'Show me
again.'

When you thought about it, it was very funny. I made my
nose into a beak, loosened my mouth and got rid of my chin,
then I thrust my arms out and stiffened my back into the
English dancing position. 'I say, may I have this dance?'

'No, actually,' my cousin Ebun said, and, whooping with
laughter, we collapsed on the bed together.

I fell in love with Akin Williams at once. He remembered me,
he said, from Sisi Bola's wedding. In the photograph, he said,
if I wanted to check, I was sitting in the middle of the front row
and he was second from the end on the left. How could I
resist? My mother asked me if he were like his father. She said
his father was tall, and when he was young, slim; not
handsome exactly, but he had a marvellously deep sexy voice.
That was Akin, I said. Akin shared a flat with my cousin
Ebun's boyfriend Olu and two others, officially that is. In
reality there were at least four others permanently resident, an
equal number passing through, and then some.

They were mostly Nigerian young men except Jamsher who
was Indian, and Kamran from Persia. Fortunately the flat,
which was on the first floor of a house in Hampstead, was
appropriately huge. Although furnished in regulation drab,
the rooms always wore a festive look because most of the
surfaces were draped in diaphanous blue and green and

yellow as if a dance of the seven veils were being continuously performed. These were Jamsher's turbans spread out to dry. The girlfriends on the other hand came from all over the globe; Africa naturally, but also from South America, the Middle East, the Far East, and every single country in between. We reckoned that there was not an au pair in London who did not pass through the flat at some stage during her stay in London. Kamran specialised in them; his tongue was smoother than Shiraz wine and his curls hung over his forehead like grapes on the vine; if he or anyone else for that matter spotted a particularly pretty one through the window, Kamran would dash down the stairs and, either on his own account or someone else's, charm her in from the street. But none of us girls actually lived at the flat, we only visited, we went home every night even if it was six o'clock in the morning.

Home was either my mother's house or Derin's house. Derin McKenzie, also a bridesmaid at Sisi Bola's wedding, was my other special friend from Lagos. As she was quick to remind me, she and I and Ebun had sworn undying friendship all those years ago in Grandma's sitting room before I left for England. Derin said her grandmother had bought a house in London only so that she and Derin's mother could keep an eye on her, now she was out of school, studying in London (which everybody knew was fraught with temptation for nicely brought up Nigerian girls) and no longer languishing in the impenetrable English countryside. Derin's mother and grandmother were also keeping an eye on Ebun, whose mother was not in England and three others in a similar position and attending the same secretarial school: Parminder from India, Shirin from Persia and Sylvianne from Belize. Derin, like me, was studying law. The six of us, former inmates of children's holiday hotels, were inseparable; the wonder, as we said, was that we had not met before this.

Ebun said, and we all agreed, that it was fantastic to wake up in the morning wherever you were and see a face that looked like yours and was not your reflection in the bathroom mirror. We moved, always in a group, between my house, the flat in Hampstead and Derin's house in Kensington. We kept clothes and possessions at each place. After years of being outsiders the thrill of belonging made us irrepressibly light-hearted; lightheaded, Derin's mother said. We dressed to look alike deliberately and we didn't care who stared at us now, protected by our identical beehives and dark glasses. When asked who we were and where we were from, we smiled mysteriously and moved on, languidly swinging our hips, all of us in our high, high heels and our tight, tight skirts.

Sandra Dee? Who she? Derin asked, amidst much laughter. My mother's house was full again, and we had turned her bedroom into a dressing room, applying the finishing touches to our appearance in front of the long mirror on her dressing table before going out for the evening. Our colleges had broken up for Christmas, which in my case was fairly academic, my mother pointed out. Disloyally, Ebun agreed with her. I attended my law lectures so infrequently, she said, I still had problems finding my way to them.

'One thing's for certain,' Parminder said, as like a swarm of iridescent dragonflies, we darted down the stairs and into the breakfast room for the approval of my mother and sisters home from school, 'Sandra Dee couldn't dance the cha-cha-cha like this!'

With a flourish we swirled our skirts and swept into a spontaneous routine which naturally we had practised to perfection.

'Bravo,' my mother said.

'You've been practising,' my sister Aduke said.

We were still breathless when Akin and Olu came to collect us in their cars. The party that night was at the house of the Western High Commissioner, and everyone would be there. When we arrived the house was so bright it was like a flare in the dark and you could almost see the walls vibrating with the music. We followed the music along the red carpet through the crowds piled up in the corridor richly wrapped like Christmas parcels, until we reached the source. In the huge reception room, the older women sat on chairs, like pictures placed against the walls, swathed in silver tissue and cloth of gold, decked out in all their serious jewellery, watching the dancing. My brother, standing with some friends, waved to me from across the room.

'Everybody's here,' I said to Akin as we crossed to join him.

'Yes,' Akin replied, looking around. 'We have survived, and very soon we can all go home.'

Presently I abandoned them and walked onto the floor to join the girls. How we danced. The music poured through our veins and we flowed with the beat. The wheel had come full circle. We wound and unwound our bodies seamlessly as if we had no bones. Is there a sight more beautiful, the older women said, than a Yoruba girl dancing?